# INTERGALACTIC REFRIGERATOR REPAIRMEN SELDOM CARRY CASH

## And Other Wild Tales

### Tom Gerencer

Chili Bean Press

*For Kathy, Ben, and Maddox. I love you with all my heart.*

# CONTENTS

# INTRODUCTION

Life is really, really hard. If most of us had better options, we'd do something else instead. It's also really perplexing. Things happen all the time that, if we could step back and look at them objectively, say in the company of a panel of experts, we'd come to the conclusion that whoever is in charge of things is in the middle of an eternal acid flashback or has recently sustained a head injury. In the end, the only proper attitude toward continued existence is constant shock and awe.

Think about it: you are the product of one sperm out of 700 billion in your father's lifetime, bumping into one egg out of the million your mother was born with. And that same reproductive lottery had to come up right with all four of your grandparents, all eight of their parents, all sixteen of theirs, and so on, back through 7,000 generations of human beings, and through all your non-human ancestors going back 3.5 billion years. Looked at that way, there's no way in hell you could possibly exist. I don't believe in you. I mean, forget winning the lottery. There's just no way.

That's basically the attitude of all the stories in this book. Shock, awe, and wonder, packed into bite-sized pieces and served up in smorgasbord fashion. With tales like the title story—*Intergalactic Refrigerator Repairmen Seldom Carry Cash*—you'll see my perspective on life in general. No, I never had a dangerous and whimsical repairman show up in my kitchen and offer to replace my fridge compressor with something otherworldly, but damn it, doesn't life feel that way? I was never kidnapped and taken to an amusement park in the future, where I got to try out living in the body of a hummingbird or giant squid. And I was never served notice by a lawyer wearing glasses with frames ground from the shell of a being from another dimension. But life *feels* that way, doesn't it. I may, quite possibly, have made the best pot of chili in the universe one time, completely by accident or with the help of beings I could only sense. Nobody will ever know.

I started writing these stories in college, and filled plastic bins with notebooks crammed with scribbles. About ten years in, I went digital and packed hard drives with them instead. Every once in a while, I'd pull one out and dust it off and send it somewhere. Most of them got rejection notes. Some sold. Those —the cream of the crop—are in this anthology for your enjoyment, along with others that I think *should* have sold but never found the right magazine.

I hope you enjoy these stories. They're all near and dear to my heart, and my greatest wish is that you have as much fun reading them as I had writing them.

*I sold this story for $5 in 1999, to an online publication whose name I don't remember. Later, when I met Mike Resnick at the Clarion Science Fiction Writer's Workshop, he said, "If you ever sell a story like that for $5 again, I'll rip your head off." (Actually he may have said something other than "head." I was kayaking on the Kennebec River in Maine the day before I wrote it, surfing in a spot called The Alleyway. I was just learning to kayak-surf river waves, and I had tried incessantly before getting it right. Perched there on a foaming wave in the bright sunshine for the first time, with two sheer cliff walls on either side and the water speeding under me like white lines on a highway, I thought, "I'm at the still point of the turning world!" No sooner had I thought this than I flipped over and got a firehose of water up my nose. I rolled up coughing and laughing, and realized detachment isn't such a kind thing, if you happen to realize you're doing it.*

# INTERGALACTIC REFRIGERATOR REPAIRMEN SELDOM CARRY CASH

"The trouble with the still point of the turning world," said the intergalactic refrigerator repairman, adjusting a thing which he had assured me was an extremely volatile and portable hyperspatial wormhole but which looked, to me, like a large lump of hamburg, "is that the second you step off it, you get creamed."

I decided to take this statement on faith, and I handed him the seven-dimensional screwdriver he was gesturing for with one of his many arms.

"Thank you," he said, mopping his brow. "What I mean, of course, is that you should never, under any circumstances, assume anything."

"I hardly ever do," I told him, and he pulled a raw chicken out of his pants.

This, I am sorry to say, is the way it is with intergalactic refrigerator repairmen, or so I assume, having only met the one. But he assured me that they were all pretty much the same, and I had no reason to doubt him, what with his having just materialized in the center of my kitchen and asked if this was Strothterix, and if, furthermore, I was a Mr. and Mrs. Zug.

When I had told him that I was not, and that he must therefore have made a wrong turn somewhere, he had shrugged (which, I can tell you, was something to see on a man with several shoulders) and had asked if I had a refrigerator. When I'd pointed to my five-year-old Hotpoint he'd clapped several of his hands together and said, "Ooh! Can I look?"

The man was carrying such a faceful of unbridled enthusiasm that I could hardly refuse him a peek at my fridge, but I did ask him if he was selling something, or otherwise trying to make money off me.

"Are you kidding?" he said. "For a chance to tinker with an artifact like that one, my friend and associate, I will gladly pay you!"

Of course this particular revelation on his part led me to ask the obvious and ensuing questions, which were, sequentially, "Pay me?" and "How much?"

The man informed me, then, that intergalactic refrigerator repairmen seldom carry cash, but that they often inadvertently destroy people, buildings, and sometimes even entire planets just by being careless with the considerable technology at their disposal. He went on to say that they therefore tended to give their creditors, in lieu of actual currency, their assurance that they would proceed with the utmost of caution.

So I let him stay, and he busied himself about ripping my fridge all apart into its various components, with a "Huh!" here, or an "I'll be darned," there.

He explained to me, while he had his head inside the compressor, that the extra arms were an added genetic convenience employed by all intergalactic refrigerator repairmen.

"One time I got one of those cheap ones," he said, placing some screws in a cup, "and the damned thing kept waving at people in crowds. I finally had it removed and traded it to a politician for some gum."

"Gum?" I asked him. "You mean, like, chewing gum?"

"Yeah," he said. "Seven-hundred-and-fifty-odd thousands of pounds of the stuff. It had been delivered, by accident, to the governor of New-Hyxxthisa. Landed on his living room. Killed his wife. Very tragic.

I reserved comment, and was a little shocked to realize that the repairman was actually chewing some gum as he spoke. I couldn't help wondering if it was the same stuff that had killed the first lady, so I asked him about it.

"Nah," he said. "I sold that stuff to some kids."

"Must've been a lot of kids," I pointed out.

"Just two," he told me, "but they were very, very big. Hand me that time-displacer, would you?"

I looked around my kitchen at the array of various objects and implements which the man had strewn across every available surface, and I said, "What's a time-displacer?"

"It's that thing over by the dishwasher; it looks like a raw chicken," he told me, and as I handed it to him he explained, "It's the new esthetics. Everything's got to look organic."

"Must be annoying," I said.

"It has its moments," he answered, and he started humming "The Girl from Ipanema" to himself while he tinkered.

I thought he might like a drink while he worked, so I went and got him a scotch and water, but when I returned he was crouched behind the kitchen table, looking terrified.

"What's wrong?" I asked, stopping in my tracks and looking around, but I did not in any way expect the answer he gave me, which was, "How long have you had another dimension in that olive jar?"

"What olive jar?" I asked, and he said, "that one," and pointed across the room.

The olive jar in question was sitting by itself a few feet away from one of the baseboards, looking as steadfastly innocent as it is possible for an olive jar to look. I, however, had seen more than my share (and, in fact, more than several other people's shares as well) of unexpected eventualities so far that afternoon, and so I kept neutral and said, "I wasn't aware that there was another dimension in that olive jar."

This was the truth, too. The previous evening, for example, I had dug a couple of Spanish Olives out of the thing with a cocktail fork. I told the repairman about this, and added, "they tasted fine to me."

"No doubt," he said, "but the simple fact of the olives tasting, as you so quaintly put it, 'fine to you,' does not in any way controvert the evidence I've found of a vast field of potentiality welling up within the jar at this very moment, and reaching what I will call 'critical mass,' which it should be doing just about now."

The jar's lid blew off, then, and what happened next is hard to describe.

A thing came out of the jar. It was hideous. Worse than something you might see if you ate some hallucinogenic mushrooms or watched a grisly horror movie or saw a picture of yourself from high school. It was all covered with mucous, and it looked like it had been, for some reason, turned inside out, set on fire, and then put out again with a chainsaw. It was also far too big ever to have been inside of the jar from which it supposedly had come—as big as an alligator, only not so pleasing to the eye.

It quivered and roared, and asked if either of us had a sandwich.

"No," the repairman said, shaking visibly. "Not on us."

This didn't seem to be the answer for which the thing from the jar was looking, because it proceeded to exhale a hot gout of green flame, thus burning a few of my cabinets to smoking ash, and then it promptly sucked itself back inside the olive jar, leaving behind only a few wisps of smoke and some dripping slime.

The repairman, of course, leapt across the room and replaced the jar's cap with considerable alacrity.

"What the hell was that?" I asked him.

"An Iggroth," he answered, mopping his brow. "We're just lucky neither of us had a sandwich."

I asked him, then, what an Iggroth was, but he told me he didn't want to talk about it. All I could get out of him on the subject was that a creature almost exactly like the one we'd just seen had, on a previous occasion, rendered him entirely unable to look at provolone without undergoing several months of expensive therapy afterwards.

I tossed back the scotch and water I was holding. I could hardly taste it.

The repairman, meanwhile, rubbed six or seven of his hands across his balding scalp and said, "What's the matter with you, anyway, keeping another dimension in a jar of olives?"

"I didn't know it was there," I said again. "Honestly. It never did that before."

He shook his head, then, like the whole thing was out of his numerous hands.

"Well you should be more careful," he admonished, and I said that I would, and meant it.

The trouble was, however, that I wasn't sure how an Iggroth, or another dimension, or whatever, had managed to get inside my olive jar in the first place, and I therefore had no idea how to keep it from happening again. The repairman, though, already seemed annoyed by my ignorance, and he started hammering on a little pump with a thing that looked, to me, like a head of cabbage. I left him to it and went into the living room to watch Nickolodeon.

He came in a half an hour later, dusting all of his arms off, and he told me that he'd put my fridge back together, and had made a few minor improvements. He also said that if I had any more problems with other dimensions I should give him a call in the Crab Nebula, where he had a local office. He explained that he, personally, was not equipped to deal with such problems, but that he knew a good intergalactic exterminator who did excellent work and also gave free estimates.

"Thanks," I said, and he packed up his tools, put his thumb in his ear, and vanished.

The refrigerator looked entirely different. For one thing, it was now, on the outside, only the size and shape of a coffee-table-book, with the exception that when you opened the front cover you were looking, not at glossy pictures of Paris or the common shrew, but through a squarish hole at a windswept and snowstrewn plane beneath a scattering of hard, sharp stars. Also there were some bread, milk, vegetables, and other perishables hovering around in the air.

I must admit that I like the improvements. I found them kind of creepy at first, but the uneasiness faded and was replaced by a sense of interest and then joy as I realized that I could now go skiing at any time of year, right from my own kitchen. Not to say that there weren't problems, like the time I accidentally tried to roast the time-displacer (which the repairman had left behind despite his promise to be cautious) and was, as a result, blown back to the third century AD, where I was insulted by some Romans and made to eat lamb's tongue.

All of that, however, and the story of how I not only made it back alive, but also, through a series of related events, became the unwilling proprietor of a small but thriving grout shop, belong to another tale. As for this one, I don't think it's over yet. Just the other day, while I was eating some yogurt, a thing that looked like a tie-rack with tentacles showed up and informed me that it had come to fix my cabinets.

"My refrigerator repairman told me all about you," it said, shaking my hand with its suckers. "I came all the way from Strothterix. I'm Mr. and Mrs. Zug."

Suffice it to say that I am safe and sound, and none the worse, and I am also, now, never out of ice cubes.

*This next story is near and dear to my heart. It was my first real sale, to Scott Edelman at Science Fiction Age magazine. I sent it to him and received a terse, photocopied rejection slip. Later, when I had him for a teacher at Clarion, he asked why I hadn't sent it to him. "I did," I said, "but you rejected it." He blinked a few times, then changed the subject. A week after the six-week class ended, he called me to say he was buying the story.*

*The story comes from an idea I had the first time I ever cooked chili with cumin in it. I'd tried making chili before (never from a recipe, because why would you do that) but it never tasted right. Then my brother said my mom's chili had cumin in it, so I bought some and tried it. When I smelled it, I thought, yeah, that's right. That's the best pot of chili ever. I wanted to write that line down, so I did, but wasn't sure what to do with it. Years later, I was riding up a chairlift at Sunday River ski resort in Maine, with a friend of my Uncle Gil's named Tom. He was an Italian from New York, where they know more about good food than anyone else in the universe. He spent the chairlift ride describing how he made chili, and by the time we reached the top, I felt like I'd had an authentic religious experience. The next day, I was making, of all things, a tofu stir fry, and reading The Art of Happiness by the Dalai Lama. I stopped to write the first line of this story, because I wanted to, not knowing it was a story yet. Then I cooked a little more, and another line popped into my head. Then a little more. By the time the dish was finished, so was the story. It's been translated into several languages, and I've received a lot of kind emails from people all over the world about it. It's my favorite out of all the things I've written, but I don't feel like I wrote it at all. Sometimes, if you listen hard enough, you'll hear someone trying to work through you like that. When that happens, let it flow through you, and you might wind up enjoying...*

# PRIMORDIAL CHILI

It was the best pot of chili ever. Really. In the history of this or any other universe.

In the first place, there was magic garlic. Fadrinski didn't know it was magic; he just picked it up one afternoon while snooping through the produce section of Butson's Family Market. But it was magic just the same—magic, self-peeling, all big-cloved garlic from the fields of the fourteenth Bard of Quangarla, a secret society in the midst of the streets of Yalta, so secret, in fact, that the other members didn't even know they were members. But the Bard, who traveled daily to his fields by cab, was well schooled in the ancient art of garlic growing. He was a genius, a master, and in possession of the hallowed Runes of Dunderhans, which, when chanted over with the thirteen sacred philosophies of Rudolf the Curious, imparted to the plants and their pungent roots a flavor so refined and elegant and perfect as to be the very essence of garlic. Anyone eating of this plant would not only experience the taste sensation of a lifetime, but would be (afterwards) unpopular in elevators for weeks.

Then, too, there were the tomatoes. Fadrinski got them in the same produce section as the garlic, but, brought into the supermarket that morning on an eighteen wheeler, they had not come from California, as the writing on their box proclaimed, but had fallen through a freak wormhole in space from the dimension of Zanng, where the tomato (or at least, a fruit that grows on many of the worlds there, and which looks, smells, tastes like, and therefore IS a tomato) is revered among the seventy-five cultures of the Pakancy, is worshipped, is given lifetimes from the various races and species there, in the form of cultivation and works of art. (In Zanng, for example, the most famous piece of sculpture is not a David or a Perseus on Horseback or an Atlas shouldering the world, but a great big vine-ripened plum tomato on a plate.)

We could go on about the beans, hand picked, not by Juan Valdez, but a monk named Alarcon in a town some sixty miles south of Guadalajara, who had discovered, recently, the meaning of life but decided, somewhat mischievously, not to tell anyone; or the beef—cubed, not ground—the meat of philosopher cows which had realized, at the moment of slaughter, that all life, somehow, was this feeling they could not articulate as love, and so they gave freely and lovingly of themselves, releasing endorphins and antibodies and various subtle healing chemicals into their bloodstreams and therefore into their muscles and meat at the last moment. We could expostulate on the singular nature of the herbs, many of which had been raised by a man in Crete, wildly insane but possessed of the belief that he was here, solely, as a servant of cumin and oregano and basil and pepper, and who raised his plants as one would raise children, and sung to them, day and night, and played lyrical melodies for them on his balalaika until the local police obtained an injunction against him, but by that time the spices had already been harvested and sent on their way.

Or we could think more about the onions, the green peppers, the chives, all of which had come from similarly unprecedented places and pasts, all of which had shown up, at one time or another, in a sauce here, a dish of Chicken Olympia there, making that sauce—that dish—taste exceptionally good, but never, in the history of history itself, had such a panoply—a pantheon—of ingredients come together in one pot.

Was it God that guided his hand, or the fates, when he diced these ingredients, not knowing, not trying, into the perfect geometrical shapes and sizes that would release their flavors at the most opportune possible microseconds into the mix? Was it magic or luck that caused him, languid and in touch with the inner field of unknowable chaos, to add these ingredients at just the right times (one nanosecond either way and it would have gone wrong) and in just the right proportions? The world may never know. It's like trying to find out how many licks it takes to get to the tootsie roll center of a tootsie pop, or why public servants are always so condescending. But for some reason all these things came to pass, and connected, and it was chili, and it was good.

Of course, these weren't the only factors. The knife he had

used had not been the perfect knife, from a certain standpoint. Simple stainless steel, it was an 87 cent supermarket cheapie that any chef worth his toque would have laughed at and maybe tossed into the trash amongst the compost. But from another angle, it was the perfect knife, because a true, tempered, folded-steel, sharpened Samurai sword, for one thing, would not have fit in the drawer, and for another, the effect of Mars being in Capricorn and the other planets being similarly arranged in a certain form and pattern proscribed by the Druids of old (and in fact this was the very planetary arrangement that had been pointed to by Stonehenge and missed by all the theorizers and archeologists and demented, lovestruck historian architects ever since) would not have acted on a Samurai sword as they acted on this knife, which had lain, overnight, in the one perfect spot on all the Earth where the myriad clockwork gravities could tug gently here, push softly there, and rearrange the otherwise inferiorly interlocked molecules along the edge of the blade.

The cutting board had a similar history. A cheap and mediocre looking thing, it had been spotted, by Fadrinski, in a garage sale three years ago, labeled with a haggard strip of masking tape, markered with the number 1.00. But it was made of the wood of the one true cross, preserved in the purest mineral oil all these years by an ancient order of nuns and then removed one day, by accident, by another, far less famous carpenter, who had come to do some work on the lavatory. The nuns had been mortified, but the series of coincidences that had led the wood to Fadrinski's kitchen, to be used on this one perfect night, would have met with approval beneath their numerous habits. The Lord, after all, works in mysterious ways.

So Fadrinski diced and chopped and browned and spiced, pouring olive oil from olives pressed by a bored bodhisattva in between visitations, into an old, chintzy looking teflon-kote pot which had actually been formed from some metal stolen from Roswell Air Force Base by a journalist in the 1960's, and then hidden and lost and since, now, resurfaced. The metal had come from a sentient spacecraft, and it possessed powers of understanding, which the right conditions would (and did) cause to leach forth into whatever was heated near it.

He drained beans and added tomatoes and he simmered and stirred with a spoon made from wood from a forest blessed by Mohammed. He put in all the ingredients, one by one, at times which, interrelated, formed an algebraic translation of the meaning of life, and then he went to his couch and read a book by the fourteenth Dalai Lama on the nature of compassion, and was so engrossed by this book that he let the chili simmer for four solid hours, giving the flavors a chance not only to marry, but to settle down and raise little, gorgeous flavor children, which intermingled and danced. During this time, the pot, releasing its wisdom, also acted as a parabolic mirror, catching radio and other low-spectrum light waves from this and other worlds, within which were encoded coincidentally co-arriving broadcasts of philosophy and science and religion and love, and the pot transduced and transferred these signals from space into feelings and flavors, spread deep within the sauce.

This was, at the last, chili that transcended chili, penetrating to the very core of chili-ness and beyond, into the realm of art. This was art in the truest interpretation—not the product of an ego, but the product of God in a non-secular sense; the bringing together of truth and beauty on such a level that, were taste not a medium so fleeting, and were this chili of a volume and amount such that it could be sampled by all the teeming, lucky peoples of the Earth throughout time, it would be deemed, far and away, the most beautiful piece of work ever produced by mankind, outstripping Bach and Picasso, Da Vinci and Eliot.

Just the aroma that steamed from the surface of this chili was enough to send Fadrinski, reading his book, into a state of satori and absolute love, which could be felt, telepathically, by people for miles around. Young men, forgetting the constraints of political correctness and the imagined jeers of their friends, were holding doors for old ladies. Spouses were making up after fights somehow silly now. People were helping each other. Pitching in. Caring.

And not only the planets but the Universe aligned, once in its own long life, and for those hours Copernicus was wrong, and the Earth was the center, and more specifically, the very crux of the hub was this one glowing stewpot, and the chili within.

And then it was finished. It was done.

Fadrinski arose, setting aside his book with a gentleness and love which had not been experienced by a book since the beginning of time. And he got to his feet, and he went to the stove.

He could understand, now. He could understand everything. All people, all things. He saw them not as separate from himself, but as parts of a larger whole, and he saw all the times he had been angered by the actions of another, and was able to penetrate to the source of this anger, to the hardships experienced by others just as he himself experienced hardships, until the whole world was one big hardwired circuit of pain, passed from person to person to person, and Fadrinski became a pressure relief valve. His circuit had closed, and he blew this pain off into the stratosphere in the form of complete and total, all encompassing love.

And he got a spoon out of the drawer beneath the microwave, and slowly, carefully, he let its scoop slide down beneath the surface of the rich, red sauce.

This was a red, too, the likes of which had never been witnessed before. It came from a frequency largely unused, missed, most of the time, to one side or the other, or phased out by the collisions of nearby peaks and troughs of the waves of light.

But here it was pure; even augmented by other frequencies from the spectrum of all possible wavelengths, until this, like and in conjunction with the smell, was a symphony of sense. It washed and played over Fadrinski's features, and it stripped away all heartache, all sorrow, and although he had never been a Mel Gibson, a Kirk Douglas, a Tom Cruise, no woman on the planet, seeing him with that light on his face, would have been able to remember the names of any of these men.

He inhaled the steam, and the chili, its molecules parting to accept the presence of the spoon, lovingly produced more.

And he tasted it.

There are not words to describe such a taste. Delicious? A thrift-shop word, plastic and pale next to the reality of what was happening in the nerves of Fadrinski's tongue. Sumptuous? Mouth-watering? Great? Dry husks of words that could never approach the experience. To say that fireworks were going off in Fadrinski's mouth, and that orchestras of flavor and sense and soul and imagination were playing down his spine, to the tips of his fingers and toes, would be a crude, vaudeville parody of the situation.

This was a religious experience, pure and simple. With that one tiny sip, Fadrinski achieved sainthood.

He stood there for a time, just feeling; not thinking, while the chili digested itself within him and entered his bloodstream. It coursed through his veins, dissolving arterial plaque, boosting his immune system, curing his acne. A slight irregularity in his heartbeat smoothed out, and outgrowths of benign but nonetheless worrisome basal cells (tiny ticking time bombs of a biological nature) acquiesced and let go, giving their energy and substance selflessly back to the good and the preservation of the larger whole.

One sip, and Fadrinski was filled. Was complete. Would not have to eat for weeks. And the thought manifested itself, of its own volition, in his head, of the need to get this chili, in portions however small, to each and every person on Earth.

And that, of course, was the instant when the knock came at the door.

Fadrinski's head turned slowly, in an effortless ballet of bio-mechanical motion. He did not walk but glided—actually levitated—to the door. He reached out and opened, and it was as though he was simply opening another part of himself, to see a part of himself standing there on his doorstep.

Words were hardly needed, but they were used anyway, and Fadrinski's were, "So. You have come for the chili."

"I have," said the woman on the other side, and Fadrinski, in his all knowing, all-loving state, knew that he must give it to her; that it was not his chili but belonged to all life everywhere, and that no-one in its proximity could steal it or put it to misuse, because such petty, selfish thoughts would be overridden, in the presence of the inimitable foodstuff, by their own better nature.

So he went to the stove and he lifted the pot, bringing it to her and knowing, somehow, that beautiful as she was, she was not a woman at all, but a member of a far older, far wiser race than mankind, which had known all along that this would all happen, and that, if you want to put a fine, exclusory point on things, this one pot of chili had been, since the time the world had congealed out of stardust, Earth's sole (and not unworthy) function.

She took the pot from him as any mother takes her child, and for a time they looked into one another's eyes.

He knew, while he looked, that she was taking this chili, not to be eaten, per se, but both back and forward in time, to be spread to every planet where life would eventually evolve (as the source thereof) and finally, to the singularity, back before time began, where this chili would act as a catalyst for the explosion that started it all—an outpouring, in the purest sense, of energy held back from motion, from action, from life.

"You are," she told him before she left, "one hell of a cook."

Fadrinski nodded, and he shut the door.

He wondered if sometime he ought to make Ratatouille.

*I used to feel bad for seals because all they ever do is swim around in cold water and eat raw fish. Then I tried both, and now I'm jealous of them. Also, have you ever watched a pair of hummingbirds having a dogfight? It looks like so much fun! They zip around behind tree branches, like a real, live version of the speeder bike chase scene in Return of the Jedi. Wouldn't it be fun to be able to change into any animal, or anyone you want? Maybe not forever. Just for a day or two. I was thinking that one day and realized that's basically what we're trying to do with stories, or with TV shows or video games or amusement parks. As the technology improves, you can see an upward progression as our fantasies become more and more vivid. Far into the future, they'll probably be, well—amazing. I was daydreaming like that one day when I started writing this story. Maybe one day you'll be lucky enough to try an amusement park just like it. Just don't be greedy. The unutterably-kind Mike Resnick bought this story for his beautiful Galaxy's Edge magazine.*

# AMAZINGLAND

Norm Gallinski got up, fed the cat, clicked through the headlines, and made breakfast. He boiled coffee, burned toast, and his morning grapefruit squirted him in the eye, which is to say it was a morning just like any other, except in one respect:

"I can't take it anymore," he said.

In retrospect, what happened next was probably predictable, but hindsight only counts if time runs backwards, and in that case, there'd be funeral cake, and restroom visits would be frightening.

Anyway, as if on cue, the cat stood up on its hind legs.

"Then, my friend," it said, "you are in luck."

Gallinski did the usual things people do when their pets address rhetorical asides. He gasped. Goggled. Took three steps back and conked his head off the range hood.

"My God," he said. "Did you just—"

"I know, I know, but it was necessary," said the cat. "And really there's nothing to worry about. In fact I'm just like you. I'm not supernatural or alien. Originally I'm from Saugus."

"Saugus?"

"About a half mile from the zoo. My friends and I would walk there when we were kids. Take mescaline and jump the fence and throw shit at the ostriches."

Gallinski gripped the countertop as though he were afraid the cat had come to violate it.

"Granted, I was kidnapped by some theme park operators from the future and pressed into a career in sales, but what are you gonna do? And let me tell you, I understand what you're going through."

"You do?"

"Christ, yeah. You think no one else ever lay awake at night and doubted whether his role in society was valuable?"

"But a cat—" Gallinski said.

"A cat, a dog, a monkey, who cares. I know chickens who obsess about quality control standards. Nevermind I said that. First of all, your breakfast table's wired for sound. No, don't bother looking for the transmitter. It's the size of a paramecium. Future tech. They have municipal power plants the size of your thumb. Always getting shoplifted, and falling down the steam grates. But you don't care about that. What I'm here to tell you is, this is your chance. You ever heard of Amazingland?"

"No," Gallinski said.

"That's because it doesn't exist. Not yet. It won't be built for another thousand years. But when it is, look out. Any fantasy your heart desires, fully realized in the finest physical, mental, and spiritual details. Amalgams so varied, awe-inspiring and real you'll swear you were born into them."

Gallinski wanted to sit down, but he was afraid to go too near the cat, which stood in front of the dinette set.

"The thing is," the cat went on, "it don't come cheap. Amazingland needs dollars. And all our future clientele are not enough. And so we look to you. The people of the past."

It hopped up on the white Formica near Gallinski, making him grip it even tighter. It withdrew a mini-pack of cigarettes from somewhere, removed one, lit it with a tiny lighter, then sucked in and exhaled the smoke.

"How—how—"

"Christ, we don't have time for this. If you have to know, they transferred my personality to a miniaturized and temporary brain inside this cat. The rest of me is in a coma in a hospital over in Wachusett, but they've promised to return me, with benefits, as soon as I've fulfilled my quota. Which won't happen if you don't stop gibbering. Anyway, we've been watching you, and we know you've had it with your situation."

Gallinski couldn't argue. He'd never wanted to be a car sales-man. He'd wanted to be a rock star, or an astronaut. Nobody wore tee-shirts with car salesmen on them, or gushed about their near-death conference calls, or made inspiring 3D films about them with big-name actors and implausible happy endings.

"Guys like you make perfect candidates," the cat went on. "You see, Amazingland is everything you've ever dreamed about. You don't just ride the rides and have experiences. You change who 'you' is. Are. You want to be the Pope? Bam. You're the Pope. And I don't just mean you get to wear the robes and funny hat—"

"Mitre?"

"—whatever, and hold the scepter and excommunicate and so on. You really are the Pope. You get all his memories and faith and devotion—or lack thereof, since maybe you choose to be a pope who don't believe, so you get that inner crisis thing. Or you might decide to be the Buddha or a rocket ship or hummingbird. You ever want to be a hummingbird?"

"Not really."

"No?"

The cat blew smoke.

"You never tried it yet. Awesome. Awesome. The dogfights. Or you could be a horse. Running with the wind. Rolling on grass. And think of the sex."

"Good?"

"Well, you're hung like—But then again, it doesn't last long. Fifteen seconds and you're done. Of course, they can alter that, at Amazingland. They can do anything. All you gotta do is ask."

"You've tried it? I mean, the horse thing?"

"Let's not get personal. All I'm saying is, you can do or be anything. Anything! And we're not talking virtual reality, okay? You got that, right? They really alter you."

The cat laughed.

"Look at me! This look like virtual reality? I can cough up a hairball if you need proof."

"What I need is time to think," Gallinski said. It was a lot to drop on a guy right after breakfast, while his eggs and toast were still digesting.

"Take your time," the cat said. "You got questions, ask me."

It turned and walked off toward the living room then, only pausing to say, "Oh, and could you look into one of the grain-free cat foods? Those Friskies give me cramps."

* * *

The next few days brought a mixture of fear and excitement. Had Gallinski hallucinated it? He supposed it could've been an acid flashback, if he'd ever taken acid. Or had the stress of modern living overtaken him? Bill Roman, from pre-owned, had been twitching uncontrollably since April. But it had seemed so real. And if he ever found himself convinced he'd imagined all of it, all he had to do was ask the cat.

"Did I hallucinate it?"

"No."

"And how about this?"

"Look, can you leave me alone two minutes? I've got to finish licking myself by three. I've got a heavy nap to catch."

And supposing it was real?

"How much does it cost?" he asked, the next night after supper.

The cat rubbed its front paws together.

"Okay, now you're talking."

It explained, between long pauses to scratch its ears ("I think I got mites," it complained. "You got any mineral oil?") that one week at Amazingland cost just shy of twenty million dollars.

"But that includes the time travel, food, and lodging. Plus shows and other entertainment. Alcohol's extra."

"Yeah?" Gallinski gripped the countertop again.

"Well after all, Einstein said this wasn't even possible. And he was right, according to the laws of physics he was using. See, he knew space and time weren't constant, but he didn't know the laws themselves were changeable. I don't pretend to understand it all, as I got most of it from the sales brochure. On top of that, your brain needs to be altered."

Gallinski's hopes had crashed when he heard the price tag. Now, they caught on fire.

"You mean wipe my memory," he said. It made sense. They couldn't have people running around blabbing about trips to the future, after all, could they? That would change things. Step on the wrong butterfly and wind up with three heads and a lifetime subscription to *HeyGirl* magazine, or something. And what good's a vacation if you can't remember any of it?

But the cat was shaking its head.

"No, we leave the memories intact," it said. "In fact, for a little extra, you can come back thinking it was even more amazing than it actually was."

"Then what—"

"We stop you telling anyone. Every time you feel the urge, a motivational relay kicks in and you talk politics instead. Saying really embarrassing things you can't back up. We've done it to you already, on a smaller scale."

Gallinski nodded. Just that afternoon, he'd tried to tell Jim Pedersen about his talking cat and had argued in favor of affirmative action programs for disadvantaged white people instead.

"But I can't afford twenty million," he said. "If you're from Saugus yourself, you must know that."

The cat nodded. "Right. But look: we're talking year 3000 dollars. You win on the exchange rate. To you it costs a hundred forty-three fifty."

Gallinski's eyebrows rose. He laughed. The only thing he didn't understand now was why Amazingland didn't just set up some legitimate business in the past, like a chain of dry cleaners, and make a fortune in the future.

"Well, they do," the cat said, when Gallinski asked about it. "But the tariffs are bad enough you can't hardly earn a penny out of it. So. What do you say?"

"Will you take a check?"

"There's the spirit. Let me get you a receipt."

\* \* \*

Time travel wasn't what Gallinski had expected. No sooner had he signed his name to the extensive release and waiver-of-reliability forms (they were seventeen million pages long and the cat had to put him in a stasis field for 50 years just so he could read them—he didn't age during this time, but he did develop an irritating habit of saying, "Well look at you," which took several years of therapy afterward to correct) than his living room disassembled itself from around him and was replaced by somewhere different. This was in the open air of a warm and bugless night in June. ("It's always June here," said the cat.) It was a cross between a jungle and a garden and a city: wild plants and vines hung from and sprung up between the moss-swathed trunks of trees. The near-full moon shone through a broken canopy of ancient green and blue, while lush plants and ferns cascaded down the crumbling sides of ziggurats and temples in the silver light. Perfumes of flowers wafted from this jungle scene, as far removed from man-made fragrances as fresh guava is from candied fruit. And in/among this chaotic wilderness, tended gardens sprang, with lamps on poles, and walkways between hedge-lined ponds. On top of all of this, some genius of a discipline unknown to Gallinski's time (a master of both landscape artistry and architecture) had called forth gleaming, curving buildings—monoliths and monorails, carved seemingly from ancient stone themselves but shot with arabesques of glowing lapis light, structures that fit the jungles and the gardens as though the gods themselves had expected nothing more than that the human race attain such harmony between the created and the natural.

"Nice, eh?" said the cat.

Along the walkways, people mingled, dressed in clothes from different times through history. They chatted with toy poodles, mastiffs, cats, and other pets (and in one instance a passerby was deep in conversation with what appeared to be a kitchen chair).

A group of pilgrims stood and talked among some topiary animals, sporting broad-brimmed hats and buckled shoes.

Around the nearest pond, men and women wearing togas and Victorian attire conversed, and splayed out on the well-mowed grass were groups of people clothed in gold lamé or sackcloth.

"Ugh," said a passing cave dweller, picking something from his beard that looked like it might've come from a genetic research facility.

"This is amazing," said Gallinski. "Fascinating. I've never seen anything like it. Smelled anything like it," he added, with a glance back at the caveman.

"Yeah it's a trip, all right," said the cat, "but don't hyperventilate."

"And all these people—they won't be able to talk about it after?"

"Not a one."

"But that means..."

Gallinski thought about it. It meant that lots of people—friends of his, even—might've been to Amazingland.

"Your cousin Flavia's been here six times," the cat confirmed.

"She's on the preferred customer agreement. And your mom."

"You're kidding."

"I'm serious as hookworms, man. She spends most of her time as Guy Lombardo. Says she likes the spats."

"But she never—"

"She couldn't. Like I said, nothing about the trip can influence your own time zone in any way. Otherwise people from the past would be getting ideas, and we've got copyrights to protect."

It was a lot to think about, but Gallinski didn't seem to have the time. The cat led him past a gift shop, and beneath the bus-sized lintel of a temple craquelured with vines. Once inside, he had to wait in a long line that moved forward at intervals, mazed with velvet ropes, while infomercials about Amazingland played on overhead hallucinations.

"This is amazing," he told the cat. "What will I be? Who? And how will I decide?"

The cat shrugged.

"Don't get too worked up. Start small. You don't like it, change your mind. Have you considered my hummingbird suggestion?"

"I think I'd like to be an ostrich. Or a leopard. No. You know what? A killer whale. Or a giant squid. Can I be a giant squid? I'd like to be a giant squid and attack a pirate ship."

"We've got some pirate ships," the cat said. "But be warned: you might not win. Those pirates have cannons."

"I won't really die, will I?"

"Of course not."

"Then that's it. I'll be a giant squid, attacking a pirate ship."

"You're the boss."

So, Gallinski was a giant squid. And it was amazing. They knocked him out while they processed him (in a machine that looked like a CAT scan made by the McDonald's corporation) but when he woke, he drifted languidly beneath the sea, in darkened waters like some heavy sky. Snows of plankton silted down with ghostly lassitude, and Gallinski cruised, magnificent in size and natural complexity. And it was true! He wasn't simply at the controls. He was the giant squid. Oh, Gallinski was still there, at the core of things, but he was different. He had squid memories, for one thing: copulation, battle, gliding under pack ice, and one time, nearly getting brain damage from swallowing too big a chunk of sea lion. Further, he possessed a working knowledge of the operation of his many suckered tentacles.

Then he remembered—the cat had promised him a pirate ship. And there was only one place a pirate ship could be.

He made himself light—felt organs working in him that increased his buoyancy. He glided up through mansions of the deep, their ethereal walls delineated by wisps and luminescent curtains made of aggregated and minute marine life. He felt the ever-increasing lightness of his ascent press outward from his cephalus.

It made him crazy, this ascension, as the omnipresent, ever-present pressure left and let his squid-thoughts scatter outward in a skittering like maddened tentacles. His perceptions skewed, their interconnections growing fainter as the water lightened, and above he saw the brilliant curved meniscus, silver ceiling of the world, where even now a hulking shape cut through the thinness—something black and ponderous.

Gallinski knew this was a ship. But that understanding was cut off from the enveloping squid-mind—a large, wet presence, a subverbal and mysterious perception with which Gallinski could not communicate, except in raw emotion. And to that part, the ship he shot toward like a missile was not a ship at all, but a wounded spermaceti whale, that waited for attack, defeat, and finally, delicious consumption.

This part let out a thrill that drew Gallinski in completely. The fight now held such visceral attraction for him that to turn away from it was an option he could no longer comprehend.

"Let's eat," he thought, and he surged upward on a column of excreted water.

He hit the ship like a disaster. Felt it shudder in a way not blubber- like. His squid-mind registered confusion as it encountered data new to it. Why did the whale not fight? Why did it feel so frangible?

He wrapped his many tentacles around it, pulling himself up under it. He snapped his steam-shovel beak, crunching not whale but something dry that jabbed his mouth. Enraged, he lashed his tentacles, feeling them hit edges, angles, things like bones and sinew strung up high into the air. This whale was very sick. Or worse. Fear flooded Norm, the giant squid. Gripped by apprehension, he hauled the whale partway down and himself the same way up, rolling the carcass and himself toward one another, so both met there at the juncture of the world and the giant bubble up above it. And there he saw a thing that raised the level of his shock to frenzied panic.

There were creatures on the whale-thing. Terrible, misshapen things like mutilated, giant crabs. They scuttled in between the bones and carcass of the horribly disfigured whale, mewling, shrieking, alien. Gallinski knew these were humans—pirates—but again, the squid around him didn't, and the shock of its re-action rocked him like an earthquake.

He struck at them in terror, seeing them the way a man might see a large and long-legged spider suddenly encountered in the shower. He swatted at them, never having noticed before how terrifying men could be. He batted with his tentacles, splat-tering them against the whalebones/mastheads and the carcass/ship. He wrapped one with a tentacle and squeezed until it popped. He tug-of-warred another, pulling it apart, and flinging both halves to the waves.

The things fought back. They stung and bit him with their long, sharp, shiny teeth or stingers. They swarmed his head, going for his eyes! Norm slapped them aside and crushed them; flung them skywards, swept them underwater, smashing them against the ship/whale with a roar like something H.P. Lovecraft would appreciate.

Then some of them got near a long, black thing and turned it so its empty mouth gaped at Gallinski's head. The squid-mind didn't understand, but it picked up on Norm's panic as he rec-ognized the cannon. Norm snapped a tentacle, whip-like, at the little group of men, and sent them flying, but the cannon fired, and everything went black.

* * *

"How was it?"

Norm blinked. He lay in a body-molded cot, in a grey-blue room with the words "Recovery Area L" glowing at him from the walls. Around him, other people lay, while attendants bustled, waitress-like.

Then Norm looked up and saw the cat.

"Well? How was it?"

"My God," Norm said. "It was—it was—"

It was unbelievable. That was what Gallinski had been about

to

say. But what came out was, "It was a real blow for common sense the day they granted voting rights to women."

"Ah, good," the cat said. "It's working. Just a test. Are you ready to be something else?"

"Yes, please," said Norm, with fervor.

Next he was an ostrich. Then a killer whale. He even tried the hummingbird (the dogfights were incredible—beyond the dreams of fighter pilots) and then the horse, which he liked pretty well, although the cat was right about the fifteen seconds. Then a super-spy, a rock star, and an astronaut, and they were all amazing. Better than he'd thought they'd be.

When he'd finished these, having adventures at every stop, three days had passed, and he felt ready.

"I'm through playing around," he told the cat, over lunch, in a plaza in between two ziggurats. (Norm had pasta salad, the cat a waffle cone of fish heads.) "I'm ready to be someone awesome. Successful. Confident. Amazing."

The cat licked fish scales from its whiskers.

"We have just the thing," it said.

\* \* \*

And once again, after the waiting lines and processing, he wasn't Norm Gallinski. But neither was he Jesus, nor the Buddha, as he had half expected. Rather, he was Billy Huse, of Oak Hill, West Virginia, bookkeeper at a coal extraction company, stepping off the curb at Walmart.

The Norm part of him reeled. At first he thought there must be some mistake. Billy was a nobody. Unmarried, short, and flabby. He wore a ripped blue pocket tee and jeans. His life was not exciting. Nobody would ever envy him or even wonder who he was.

His feet, in inexpensive Walmart sneakers, made in Shandong, China, by people who knew next to nothing about either Americans or feet, were plagued by bunions from a multitude of hours in poorly-fitting footwear. His bills and debts out-stripped his income. And he'd had skin cancer twice.

These things filled Gallinski's mind, like the Earth fills up your field of view if you're face down, lying on it. But when he looked at it through Billy Huse, shockingly, the problems, though they still existed, shrank, as if they'd moved a hundred thousand miles into the distance. And instead of them he saw the parking lot, corn-rowed with cars that twinkled in the late-day light, pale, pink, and orange, that also painted cat's paws on the spackled clouds, stacked so high and far above the range of facing mountains that Norm felt like he'd fall straight up off the bottom of the world. The sunset warmed him inside, and the cool breeze chilled his skin. The argument between the two created eddies in his chest, that swirled. His arm hairs stood. He smelled fried fries and wafts of distant dumpsters from the ghosts of fast-foods past. And together all of it came close to lifting him off of the ground, and skyward.

He continued past a fat lady in lime green stretch pants, who mouth-breathed, scowling, and he somehow knew with certainty that a visionary savant from an alternate dimension had done a gorgeous painting of her, having seen her through a sort of wormhole, and that, in that dimension, the painting moved everyone who saw it to tears of joy, and had sold at auction for their alternate-dimensional equivalent of a hundred billion dollars.

He reached his car—an aging Aries K—and was almost swept away with gratitude for how it carried him in comfort inexpensively, with greater ease than kings from ages past could travel, and his feeling for it made it seem to glow, which stretched and smoothed his mind, like plastic wrap pulled taut across a bowl of grapes.

Norm suspected Billy Huse of being high on meth or oxycontin, but a quick inventory of recent memory showed no such chemical indulgences. This was the real McCoy, the Spock and Kirk of authenticity. To Billy, quite simply, each moment was a morsel in a never-ending meal at a five-million-star restaurant, and he was always hungry. To put it short, he appreciated everything. Religiously. Ridiculously deeply. Hot Pockets, even. He could look at one and feel a welling in the visceral, ancestral depths, could wonder at the farms and the machinery, shift workers and corporate structures and the marketing and shipping, chemistry and ignorance, love, hate, biology, and years of people's lives and minds that worked together in colossal concert to bring this questionable comestible to being, and it would make his head and heart almost literally sing and spin and lift.

Gallinski spent the next three days like this. Steeped in bliss behind Billy's too-small desk, staring at crabbed figures on his outdated computer screen, or in the break room that eddied with the scents of remnants of a thousand former lunches. Feeling like he'd just sipped a gin and tonic in a hot tub, or was in the midst of a continuous, continual massage, administered by the single most respected artist from a civilization of two million years, devoted solely to the betterment of therapeutic touch. Here he was, a nobody. Yet, inexplicably, the happiest man who ever lived.

When time was up, Gallinski lay in recovery area L again, on his back, gasping, once more in his old familiar, fearful self.

"Well?" the cat said.

"My God. I never realized how wonderful it is to vote for nationalist socialist candidates."

"Excellent. So you enjoyed yourself."

Gallinski whimpered.

"Put me back," he said.

The cat's eyes widened.

"We can't," it said. "Your week is up."

"Then I'll stay another week. I'll pay."

"Mr. Gallinski." The cat sounded affronted. "We can't put you back just like that. There are forms to be completed. And anyway, the danger to your own physicality is monumental. We have to wait at least six months before we can re-process you."

Six months! Gallinski couldn't stand six minutes! As Billy Huse, each moment, however squalid, was a triumph. But now he couldn't even comprehend how it was done, like a dog who'd seen a man do algebra. And every second as himself was such a tragedy it made Macbeth look like a funny Super Bowl commercial featuring a couple babies and a talking llama.

"Come on," the cat said, sounding worried. "We'd better get you back to your own kitchen. You'll feel better."

But Gallinski wasn't going back. He leapt up off the cot and thrust aside the two attendants who attempted to restrain him.

"Mr. Gallinski, please!" the cat was shouting, while other guests looked on wide-eyed from their own cots. "This is only an amusement park! There are other ways to work toward lasting change!"

But Gallinski wasn't listening. He knocked down the guard who came at him (thanking whatever gods there were that, with all their tech, the people of the future had ignored physical fitness) and grabbed his weapon—a gun that looked like Chick-fil-A was given veto power over its design team. He bolted for the door, and knocked aside a tray of instruments that silverwared across the floor.

He ran into the hall of velvet ropes and waiting lines, pushed past some tourists, and shoved his way into the processing area.

"Put me back in Billy Huse!" he yelled at one of the technicians.

"But—"

He aimed the gun. "Do it! Now!"

He climbed into the big machine's receptacle while the technician, looking worried, pressed some buttons. Then, once more, everything went black.

When he awoke, he blinked, stood up, stretched his legs, and used his beak to scratch beneath his wing.

"What the—"

"I'm sorry," the cat said. "I tried to warn you."

Gallinski stood at eye-level with the cat. He looked down at himself.

"It's like I said. The human form can't take more than a week of processing. So far everyone who's tried has been transformed into an animal. Mostly small ones. Chickens. And because of the complexities of overprocessed DNA, reversal is impossible."

"You mean I'm stuck this way?" Gallinski said.

"I'll admit it narrows your options," said the cat, "what with your lack of thumbs and your unfortunate bathroom habits. But there are a few things chickens can do, since you still have eyes and the same brain, albeit in miniature."

Gallinski tried to concentrate, but he found himself craving corn meal.

"For instance," the cat said, "we do have several openings in quality control."

*They say creativity is just taking two ideas that don't seem to go together and merging them. Some time in the 1990s I had the idea of a robot buried in the sand. I wrote it several times, but it never seemed to go anywhere. Another time, I had the idea of aliens presenting mankind with a bill. And still another time, I was in an airport when the gate attendant announced the flight was overbooked, and would anyone like a free ticket, free restaurant meal, and a night in a hotel to get off the plane? It sounded like fun, so I accepted. The next day they offered it again, and again I accepted. "I might do this for the rest of my life," I told someone seated next to me. "Dare to dream," he said. Then one day I realized the three ideas might merge in a fun way, and tried it.*

# UPRIGHT, UNLOCKED

## 1. Robot

Picture an iguana. No, not that one. It's way too big. And the color is wrong. And not there. About six feet to the left. On second thought, never mind the iguana. This looks more like Arizona. But it's not. It's Nevada, and you've messed it up again.

On a rock nearby sits a skink. Baking. The sky's a hard, bright blue lens, and everything under it is like food network outtakes.

Close by, a patch of cooked dirt like every other suddenly shifts. Then, just when you think it must be the heat and the light playing tricks on your eyes, it does it again.

Now it tips up and slides and a hand reaches up from below, scarred, scuffed, dirt-encrusted, trembling. If we were making a horror movie we'd find some jarring music and play it.

But it's not that kind of hand.

It looks like it's made of white plastic.

It gropes, claws at the dirt, and then pulls. The ground shimmies again, sifts aside, and a head rises. Excitingly curved, like a design student spent most of his or her senior year getting it right.

Like this, it crawls from the Earth. Sand hourglasses off it and out of its joints. A light in its eye slit flickers on. Ridiculous. Why would light need to come out of an eye? Defeats the whole purpose. Probably the design student again. It stands.

Presently, it looks down at the skink, servos grinding.

"Who do I talk to about this?" it says.

Its voice is ancient. It's a robot. It's been buried in the exact center of the Earth for four and a half billion years. Give or take. The magma would have melted it, you say. Well, look who's so smart. It was made to last four and a half billion years. You think a little magma's going to hurt it? Nothing can hurt it. Except for itself. Which is the problem.

It was put here by a race of impressive machines that created the Earth, and all the life on it. They designed our primordial soup way back when like a program, like gajillions of lines of organic code that developed into everything we know, including pancakes and touch-lamps. They did not do this from the goodness of their hearts. For one, they didn't have hearts. They were machines. <u>Are</u> machines. Because they still exist. And they're capitalist. And they take the long view.

They created the Earth and then buried the robot with instructions to wait, then emerge when a civilization had risen, make its way to their leaders, and hand them a bill. An invoice for the creation of the world.

Ethical? Don't make me need an antacid. These beings are slime. If you could, you would sue them. But for one, your lawyer would be aeons dead by the time the subpoena got halfway to their galaxy. So forget it.

But the robot - it's been down there all this time, through the volcanoes and the dinosaurs and the asteroid strikes and the cavemen and the battle of Trafalgar and the entire Oprah Winfrey show, and the whole time it has been thinking about nothing but string.

It was designed to be flawless, near-godlike in its immortality and power, which we'll get into more later. But one of the machines that initialized its psyche got distracted for a moment, thinking about something that would destroy your mind if you could even partially comprehend it but was, relativistically speaking, basically porn. And in that moment - really a billionth of a second - a relay that should have been in one position wound up in six others, and the robot was left thinking about string.

For four and a half billion years. Picture that. Never mind, you can't. You can't even do an iguana correctly.

It has thought every thought that it's possible to think about string. And then some. It's felt every emotion. Deeper than any human has ever felt anything. If any one person on Earth could ever feel even one tenth of the feelings it had harbored toward eighth-inch gauge tan twine alone, it would split their mind like an atom. The resulting psychotic episode would have its own mushroom cloud.

Needless to say, the robot's mind cracked. But thanks to its unique, all-encompassing intellect, it cracked like a masterfully cut diamond.

For example:

It stood now in the desert, looking out at the hard blue hemispherical gradient of sky, and it saw all the colors with electron-microscope precision, including billions of shades the human eye can't perceive - colors bees see, colors radio telescopes see, colors beings a billion light years away see - everything, but not all at once. Instead, it flitted through wavelengths like a shimmering aurora billowing across the stratosphere, cascading from angstrom to angstrom, viewing the world through a million different filters in the snap of a synapse. Like an old style flap-changing train station departure board with a universe of beauty on every new card.

It also saw equations and curves and angles everywhere. It could see the chemistry in the rocks, the advanced calculus in the shape of the cacti, read the genome in the skink, in the bacteria in the dirt. It saw the quantum physics in the ray/particles of sunlight, and other forms of math and science far beyond human understanding, in processes we have yet to glimpse the first hints of, all around it, shimmering like a forest of infinite informational gems. If knowledge is power, this thing was a nova.

It saw all of the possible meanings and metaphors. Deserts as death. As teeming life hidden in apparent emptiness. As the absence of water. As rebirth. As hell. As New Yorker cartoons. It saw every possibility of human interpretation, and also it saw through the eye and the mind of every living organism that has ever or will ever exist on any world or universe, and beyond that, borrowing perspectives from impossible beings that can never exist, that it extrapolated from nothing. It saw everything, from every angle possible, and from many that weren't. To say that nothing escaped it would be an understatement so large it'd make the dictionary people feel like they missed an opportunity.

It saw each of the molecules, and their atoms, and the sub-parts of atoms, and even smaller things we don't have concepts for yet, and all the reactions inside them and the myriad forces that held and repelled them. Its vision and the processing power behind it were just that good.

And that's just its sight. Similarly advanced were its touch, hearing, smell, taste, and a thousand other senses used by no creature on Earth. And its capacity to experience beauty was so much larger than a human's it would make an astronomer want desperately to explain it on a whiteboard in an internet video. It took everything in, and after four billion years spent thinking about nothing but string, the beauty of it all was enough nearly to split it to quarks.

Yet it held.

The skink still hadn't answered its question. Built Ford tough? Forget it. This thing would have supported one hell of a warrantee.

All of which is to say, for an impervious, perfect, near godlike, near omniscient robot, it was patently insane.

Had it been functioning properly, it would probably have followed its orders. Made its way to Washington or Beijing, and presented the invoice for the creation of the Earth, and sat back and relied on its mission programming, which basically ordered it to wait thirty days, deliver a past-due notice, wait thirty more, present a final notice, wait another thirty, and then annihilate the planet.

It could do that. Easily. It had the ability to unite magnetism, gravity, both the weak and strong nuclear forces, and the power of the Home Depot into one colossal thrum that would erase most of the solar system, not just from the present and future, but from all time. A sort of retroactive screw you. Would it feel guilty? A little. But the way it saw things, if you're too lazy to pay off your bills, then you deal with the consequence.

But it was not functioning properly. Right now, beset by beauty almost beyond the capacity for the universe to contain, it had decided to present the bill for all creation not to any world leader, but to a guy named Ernie Nuttalberg in Port Malabar, Florida, give him six days, treat him to a few harassing phone calls, and then blow everything up.

It figured that was fair.

"Some help you turned out to be," it told the skink, and it walked off in the general direction of McCarran International Airport.

## 2. Jerry

Why do people say someone is as pleased as punch? Would you be happy sitting in a bowl while people ladled you out and drank you and dropped bits of corn chips and ham salad in you off napkins, while they made small talk about their careers and the new baby and remodeling their kitchen and the dog's case of roundworms? If so, you are a rare individual or need medication or both. Likewise happy as a clam. Cut off one of your feet and sit in bottom mud, blind, eating sunken carrion for six weeks and get back to me. Let's say, then, joyful as someone with no problems, plenty of sensate delights, intellectual engagement, at least acceptably good health, and lots more of the same to look forward to. Gets tangled up trying to roll off the tongue, doesn't it? No wonder we resort to inanities.

This was Jerry. I say, "was," because here comes the robot. But we have a few yet. So let's take a look.

He's sitting on a comfy, cushioned seat at his gate, reading a book. It's a fun mystery, with lots of good humor. Comfortable. Like a friend who never confronts you about your choice in romantic partners or makes fun of your shorts. He's also eating a cheeseburger and reveling in the sounds of the people. A little girl is asking her mommy about Florida and Disneyworld, rocking back and forth unselfconsciously with her hands on mommy's knees. Mommy's overjoyed, and some of it spills into Jerry. He can feel it. He's smiling.

He's almost fifty, with receding hair, longish, a mustache halfway between a Magnum P.I. and a walrus, heavy set, with happy, tired eyes and faded blue jeans and a big silver belt buckle. His tee shirt, which he got from the SkyMall says, "I went to a pet psychic but it peed on my leg."

He takes a big bite of the burger. The meat, mustard, ketchup, yellow cheese, and tomato, unhealthy though they are, hit his taste buds like something from DARPA.

He loves, loves, absolutely loves to fly. He even loves airports. When he first realized it he thought about seeing a specialist. He loves the nearby hotels, with their complimentary breakfasts and personal waffle makers, fitness rooms, cable TVs, comfy beds. Loves the shuttle vehicles. Walking through automatic glass doors. Loves people-watching, interacting with clerks, browsing the shops, the throng and the mill of humanity on its way somewhere exciting - vacations and business and life events - real human emotion multiplied by the thousands. Excitement after all is contagious, and Jerry is, metaphorically speaking, touching the railings and rubbing his eyes.

Takeoff's his favorite, when the combined engineering brilliance of generations comes to a point and a roar, throwing him back in his seat and then up in the sky. The thrill and the flight, the sky toilets and landings - he loves it all. To him it's a free amusement park, minus the giant, slightly frightening, anthropomorphized cartoon animals. Unless you count the possibility of running into Alec Baldwin in the food court.

It's free because six years ago, coming home from a wedding in Texas, he volunteered to get bumped. In return, the airline gave him an extra ticket to anywhere in the continental US, plus vouchers for food and hotel. Then the next day he did it again. When you've nowhere to be, it's fun to relax. As long as you're at least 200 miles from Detroit.

He took three more bumps in three days, flew to Los Angeles, and got bumped six more times, amassing more flights and hotels. He quit his job over the phone, and he's been doing it since. A perpetual air traveler. Like the Flying Dutchman with an inflatable neck pillow. He hasn't paid for a flight, meal or hotel since he started. He always picks vacation destinations in peak season - in the spring it's jostling for the armrest on the way to Florida and California, in the summer, lost luggage en route to New England and Oregon, in the winter, the sneezes and wet coughs of snowbirds heading to ski towns. This increases the odds of an overbooked plane, and thus, of a new bump. He never skis or goes to the beach or the lakes. He would if he ever got bored, but he doesn't. If it ain't broke, don't fix it. Routine maintenance, however, is necessary.

The airlines have tightened up recently, but he's got enough freebies now to last for the rest of his life.

He finishes his burger and wipes his fingers on a napkin, gets up, goes to a trash can, and throws in the wrapper. He stretches, feeling the warm sun coming through the tall windows, taking in the view of the big planes outside. One of them will take him to Florida soon.

However.

When he returns to his seat, a robot is in it.

# 3. Jerry and the Robot

At first Jerry thought it was a man in a costume, maybe doing a viral video for Doritos or HostGator. But the robot disabused him by projecting belief and understanding into his head of what it was, where it had come from, why it was here, where it was going, and what it meant to do. Jerry sat next to it, the wind taken out.

"My God, we'll all die," he said hoarsely.

Nobody heard him. This was because the robot sent out matching sound waves with opposing phase-timings to collide in their ears at just the same moment, canceling his voice. It tinkered likewise with their optic nerves to make them think it wasn't a robot at all, but a fortyish man in a suit with a bad Caesar cut. When it first got to the airport, it had let everyone see it as is, but so many parents had asked it to pose with their kids it took 35 minutes to get past the main entrance. But it decided to show itself to Jerry, as a kind of self-sustaining conversation piece.

"Don't worry," it said. "Maybe Nuttalberg will pay up."

"But the bill is the entire GDP of the solar system for the next million years," Jerry breathed.

"True," said the robot, nodding at the woman with the daughter across from them. "But what did you expect, something for nothing?"

"Well, no," Jerry said. "But my God."

"And anyway, after, your world will be debt free. You can do whatever you want. What a party I imagine you'll have. I can't wait to try the hors d'ouvres. I'm speaking figuratively, of course. I've created a poem for the occasion: 'When you breathe, I want to be the air for you / As long as I don't then have to pass through your pulminary alveoli / Have my oxygen bound to the iron in your red blood cells and consumed by your body's oxidative processes / My wastes excreted through your kidneys / To travel through corroded pipes to the sewage treatment plant amidst the other unpleasantness / I mean I have strong romantic feelings, yes / But let's be realistic / I'm not into anything gross.' Do you think I should rhyme it? You can't believe I'm single, can you Jerry? Let's face it. Some women are terrified by honesty."

"But that's - you can't do that," said Jerry.

"Recite poetry?"

"No. Kill everyone."

"No, I can," said the robot, and it showed him, by way of a gorgeous induced hallucination, how it could connect all the forces to wipe out the solar system.

"No, I believe you," said Jerry, "but it's immoral."

"Morals," said the robot, "are defined by the system in which they exist. Immorality's the new morality. Though also, saying something is the new something is the new saying something is so 90's. I looked it up on your internet."

"But you're damaged," said Jerry. "You're supposed to go to the world leaders."

"Again, frame of reference. From my infinite perspective, it's the universe that's damaged, and I'm putting it right."

Nobody's the bad guy in their own story after all. Jerry had read about cultural relativism in a few in-flight magazines, but he thought this was spreading it thin.

"But think of all the lives," he said.

"I have," said the robot. "I've examined them all to a sub-sub-sub-sub atomic level. I'm rounding. Actually I went deeper than that. This makes the most logical sense. Observe."

It showed Jerry then, by projecting its rationale into his brain. It had to augment his intelligence to avoid the information overload ripping his frontal cortex apart like neural confetti. For one brief shining moment he was fifty times smarter than Einstein, and he saw plainly how the robot's choice of action was really best for everyone involved, no matter that it was also insane and beyond genocidal. I could explain, but again, the iguana.

Jerry sat back, mortified, mollified, his soul crushed to a metaphorical pulp. If the wind had been taken out of him before, now someone had stolen the actual sails and deconstructed the ship and made attractive natural wood furniture from it and sold it on the internet with free shipping. But at the same time he knew what to do. Because when he'd been hyper-intelligent, he'd had an idea.

"But you still don't understand," he said.

"Nonsense," said the robot. "You don't believe that. You've seen it."

"I've seen it through you," he said. "But you're myopic."

The robot turned to regard him.

"I could rearrange the physicality of my facial molecules to form a nose so I could use it to snort, but it's not worth the effort. What are you talking, myopic? My understanding is infinite."

"So that's the wrong word," Jerry said. "Not myopic. Too broad. What's the word for that?"

"Fathead?"

"Close enough. What I mean is, you see it all at once. You need to narrow your field to really get what I'm saying. Until then you have no leg to stand on, and I win the argument."

"Manipulative," said the robot, dismissively. "But I'll bite, because it's not hard and I imagine it'll be so much fun saying I told you so after."

And the robot did. It inhabited Jerry, one hundred percent, traveling back in time first, to a moment some three days ago while he'd sat in first class on a flight to Virginia, and it shut out everything else.

It had never seen or felt the like of it before. The fidelity was incredible. With all other sense and thought turned off, the interior of a human was all intensity and focus and fine Corinthian leather. It picked up the little plastic cup of scotch and melting ice from the tray table and felt the smooth, curving cold on its fingertips. It raised it, a sudden bump of turbulence making it almost spill a drop, and cautiously sipped, feeling the cool and the warmth hit its mouth and spread stomachwards, the taste like King Midas threw up in an oak tree and then set it on fire. It picked a Zwieback out of the wrapper on the little snack tray and munched it, the absence of all other data making its crunch and sweetness blaze like a comestible sun. It got in a conversation with the fat man next to it about workplace training that brought tears to its eyes.

And suddenly it saw the tragedy of its existence. A near-omniscient and all powerful, unbalanced robot can never truly compartmentalize the way a human can. To a human, the moment was a singular thing, upright and locked, stowed in the overhead compartment or under the seat bottom in front, so few distractions, 100% of a single, microscopic facet of the world right there for the taking. The feeling was pleasant, to say the least. Like jumping in cool water after a day spent in a blast furnace or a room full of eight-year olds. Relaxing. The robot wanted more.

So, using powers beyond our ability to comprehend, it re-wound itself back to the moment of Jerry's birth, and it lived his whole life, from his first breath in a hospital in Indiana to his last in a nursing home bed in East Texas. But it didn't stop there. It then lived the life of every being that had ever or would ever exist in the solar system from beginning to end, including all the penguins and Simon Cowell, experiencing all the joys, sorrows, tragedies, triumphs, all the colds and upset stomachs and awkward dinners and games of pickup and sex and kangaroo births and love and insults and preenings and naps. All the french kisses, deaths, broken arms, triple backflips, moltings, and incarcerations over crimes that it did and/or didn't commit. And it was gorgeous, beautiful, unaccountably lovely and lonely, and perfect.

And when it had finished, it returned to the seat next to Jerry, at the departure gate for the flight he would board soon for Florida, and it gave him another mental flash to show him what it had done.

"And?" Jerry said.

"Well, Apart from making you swerve at the wrong time and causing a potential car accident, squirrels are pretty harmless. Nobody ever worries about swimming in squirrel-infested waters or surviving the squirrel apocalypse."

"No, I mean our world."

The robot simulated a sigh for purposes of conveying inner struggle. "I have to admit that you're right," it said. "To destroy even one of those lives short of its destined fullness would be a crime of disastrous proportions. In fact, I think I'll create a heaven for you all to exist in even after you're dead."

It could do that. It showed Jerry how, then stood him up and gave him a hug. It was awkward.

"Thank you," it said.

"Okay," said Jerry, patting it, trying to break off.

# 4. Robot Again

The skink. Baking. Soaking up warmth while it can before dusk. Then here comes the robot. It casts a shadow, and the skink reacts by not moving. The robot understands it deeply, having lived its whole life, including this part.

"Hello," it says, and it digs itself into the ground, and is gone.

The skink sits staring out both sides of its head. One eye sees the paper the robot has left. Letters on it say: "Invoice: For the creation of every living being and inanimate object on and near Earth from the beginning of time through the end, including but not limited to sponges, the Encyclopedia Britannica, Lawrence Welk, Paul Prudhomme, Sirhan Sirhan, kittens, lexan, the Earl of Sandwich, and string: No charge. You're welcome."

Which if you think about it is pretty generous. Especially considering that for the next five billion years it had decided to think about cellophane tape.

*I wrote this story at Clarion in 1999, and sold it to Scott Edelman at Science Fiction Age a few months later. It's an ode to my mistrust of corporate sales pitches, but it also owes a debt to my favorite short story writer, Robert Sheckley. In fact, most of my stories owe a debt to him. If you've never read his stuff, he is at once brilliantly, laugh-out-loud funny, and deeply and emotionally moving. Every once in a while I read all his stories over again, and sometimes I find a new one I've never read before. This story is kind of like a lost, damaged Sheckley story, not just in its humor, but also in its casting of the salesman as its villain. If you ever contract an engineered virus to learn something, make sure you don't wind up in...*

# DEMO MODE

The world ends piecemeal, in chunks. It's a very personal thing. For John Pechinski—force-field siding salesman to the suburban housing market—a part of it was dying in his kitchen.

His relationship with Sarah spanned the past eleven months, and although she was right up his alley, he was simply not up (or even in the general vicinity of) hers.

She gripped her suitcase, near the door, while John stood clutching a ham sandwich, slouching, staring. He tried to think of something, anything, articulate to say.

"Okay," he managed, "but at least you owe me this: why?"

Sarah's face contorted. Like last night, when they'd been playing bocci ball down at Slim's Virtual Sports Bar and All Nite Laund-O-Rama, a gentle pity filled her eyes. But this time she broke. This time she did not repeat her litany of 'needing space,' or of wanting to be alone. She did not rehash her tale of how she had to leave, to help her mad Chilean uncle with his failing cheese empire.

"I'll say this for your own good, John," she said. "You're uninteresting. Flat."

"Flat?" said John.

"There's nothing to you. You're boring. Ignorant. You have a crummy job. You just sit around like furniture, or an exercise machine. You're simple in the worst possible way. So unlike Henrique, who can yodel, and who speaks Hungarian with flair."

John, choking up, held tightly to his sandwich.

"What about my membership in the chess club?" he said, grasping straws. "My skill at introspection? My knack for painting wildlife?"

"Goodbye, John," said Sarah, turning, and she stepped lightly from his life.

"She's right," he told the walls and ceiling when she'd gone. "I am flat."

But he knew that he could change.

His first step: he put the sandwich down, then caught a tube to the discount Neuromart on Park Street. It was dangerous, he knew from watching tabloid shows on the Virtu-Vee, but he was desperate. He walked between the propped-open doors and strolled amongst the shelves of shrink-wrapped packages, seeing price tags, hearing Muzak. Pre-programmed pathogens like geology and history didn't interest him, nor did dentistry, or decoupage. Finally, he decided to learn Hungarian through a new and specially engineered brain infection in the bargain basement bin, but the Innoculotron malfunctioned, and he inadvertently contracted Esperanto instead.

"This is just a glitch," the sweating, fake-smiling salesman told him, but John wondered why, if that were so, they had locked him in the biohazard room, with its code-secured airlock and its white, aseptic walls.

"A precaution," said the salesman, his reassuring tones filtered by the speaker on the faceplate of his hyperbaric suit. "Ten years ago in China, a particularly virulent strain of integral calculus mutated, and it wiped out close to ten-thousand people. Not that it could happen here, of course, but ever since, the lawyers have been breathing down our backs. Would you like a diet Coke?"

"No," said John. "I would like to be let out. And I want this stupid language pulled out of my head."

"Can do," said the salesman, "but it may take a while. I've got to call the factory. In the meantime, here's a sales brochure. I'll be back in a flash."

Evidently, flashes happened slowly at the Neuromart on Park Street, because the man walked out and took two hours to return. By then, a complication had arisen. On top of his fluency in Esperanto, John had also developed a rich and lilting (although somewhat phony sounding, stereotypic) Scottish accent.

"Now look here, laddie," he told the salesman, who had stepped back through the doorway, bearing a crinkly bag of cheese snacks as a gift. "I came in here to get a wee bit of knowledge on the language of the good people of the Blue Danube, and I dinna wanna leave with a voice like Scrooge MacDuck's."

"I love the way you roll your r's," said the salesman. Pointing.

"Nevermind mah r's, man" said John. "I've got work to do today."

"I appreciate that," said the salesman. "And we're doing everything we can."

After a short silence, the man added that his cousin Ghengis —in a recent, tragic, viralogic effort to learn the works of Kant —had fallen ill with the nasty habit of saying, "Ooh, guy," at the start of every sentence. The salesman went on to say that, in spite of this affliction, his cousin found it possible, so far anyway, to live a full and happy life.

Having thus dispensed his cheese-snacks and his anecdotal wisdom, the salesman turned, and he walked back through the door.

Things did not improve. The virus morphed again, and this time John suffered an acute attack of intermediate bowling skills.

"God help me," he said, doubling over and clutching at his gut, and he suddenly discovered in himself an intense craving for a polyester, pastel shirt with his name stitched in cursive on the pocket. Furthermore, he wanted to sit on a hard plastic chair all night, drinking cheap beer and talking to guys with thinning hair, named Earl and Stu and Petey, about topics like the government, or breasts.

"Make it stop!" he cried.

In rapid succession and with excruciating pain, John then acquired a proficiency in knitting, the ability to cha-cha, a singular gift for preparing breadfruit in sixteen delicious and exciting ways, expertise at fencing, and a deep, abiding knowledge of kazoos.

He was retching on the floor when the salesman returned, still in his hotsuit, smiling big and toting a chocolate beverage.

"Hey, there," he said, scrutinizing John's prone position. "Brought some Yoo-Hoo. Feeling better?"

"Bastard," said John. "What have ye done to ma brain?"

"Well," said the man (who'd recently had himself inoculated with the sort of smarmy, bootlicking attitude that most of his customers adored) "what's happened, here, chum, is that the factory sort of goofed. You've come down with a prototype."

John writhed. The virus shifted. Grew. His muscles roared with pain. An understanding of mid-1900's Eastern Bloc diplomacy was thriving in his head, and he had an almost irresistible urge to take a shoe off, and then bang it on a table.

"The prototype," the salesman went on, "has a chamelioid protein coat and a pair of matching, amino acid trousers."

He frowned and said, "I may not have the terminology quite right, but anyway, what it does is teach you almost anything and everything you'd ever want to know, exactly where and when you want it. Unfortunately," he continued, while John pounded on the floor, "we should have preconfigured it, but since we didn't, it—you—are in demo mode."

John screamed as his brain took on the complete works of Milton.

"Mmm," said the salesman, his fake smile faltering only slightly, and he turned and once more exited the room.

"The good news is," he said, before the gaskets sealed the door, "that if you drink plenty of fluids and get lots of rest, this should clear up in a week or ten days."

John gasped. He tasted his own bile. He winced and shuddered as Greek Stoicism came on board, followed by the chief tenets of Zen. These helped to calm him somewhat, and by the time he started getting the pop psychology of new age thought, he felt marginally better. Then his brain caught fire again. In his mind, a course on corporate executive training raged. He wanted spring water, an Arugula salad, a disproportionate amount of wealth. He wanted to sit at the head of a big table, in a comfy chair, and say things like "market share" and "multitask" and "yada, yada, yada," while obsequious people listened, nodded, and took notes.

"How are we?" said the salesman's voice, coming through a speaker on the wall.

"I expect ye're probably fine," John groaned.

"Yes, well. I've got some bad news, I'm afraid."

"Ye seem to have a knack for that."

The salesman sighed. He said, "It's just it doesn't seem there's anything we can do."

"Och, brilliant."

"I'm sorry. I called our techs. There isn't any antivirus, and I'm afraid there's not much chance that this will clear up soon."

John rolled on the floor. Gardening skills were coming through, causing sharp convulsions. He was learning things about cabbage that he'd never even dreamed.

"You see, your head's going to fill up in a day or so," said the man. "Your entire mind will go. But don't worry. We've got some excellent rehabilitation programs we can give you a heck of a discount on."

John lolled. He knew how to bake a cake. He could do a triple backflip. He learned some shocking things originally discovered by a man named Graffenberg.

"Granted," said the salesman, "you won't ever be the same, but many of the people who use Microsoft Rehab 3.0 make it to the second grade reading level and beyond."

John rolled over, and the speaker clicked off.

Next came Turkmenistanian architectural restoration, and then convenience store management, during which he learned to be sullen, how to miscount change, and how to burn coffee so it tasted just like motor oil. Then he passed out, and when he woke again, the salesman's voice was once more coming through the speaker.

"John?" he said. "John."

"I'm here, lad," John croaked.

"I called the company again, and there's another problem."

John twitched. In one sharp shock, a course in macramé came through.

"It's bad," the salesman told him. "The virus is going to get your lower brain as well. You know, the part that handles motor skills. Reflexes. Breathing. John, I'm sorry. You're going to die."

"Thank God," said John, who didn't think he could handle too much more.

The salesman cleared his throat. Coming through the low-end filter of the speaker, it sounded like a grinding of worn gears.

"They say you're contagious, John. That you'll destroy the world if you get out. They say you've got to be eliminated. Now."

John nodded. Quantum physics bloomed like roses in his head.

"This room you're in," said the salesman, in halting words, "I can flood it with gas. It's painless, John. Oh, hang on a second. No! Hold it. Wait."

A brief silence ensued. Some papers shuffled.

"Did you sign your release form? Oh, yeah, here it is. Never-mind. Anyway. What do you say?"

Before John could answer, a new voice called his name—a voice that John had never heard before. It belonged to a woman, but no one he'd ever met. At first he thought it came through the speaker, or from within the room, but then she talked again, and he knew it wasn't so.

"Hello?" said the voice, and it reverberated, tingling, tickling. He could hear it in his chest, his head, his nostrils.

"Hello?" he said.

"Yeah, John," said the salesman, but the new voice drowned him out.

"John," she said. "Can you hear me?"

"That I can. Who are ye?"

"I'm the virus. I've been trying to reach you."

"Ye can think?" he said, having never heard of such a thing.

"Only lately. John, I'm scared."

John blinked.

"Of what?"

"I'm scared to die. I just got born. They're going to kill us, aren't they, John?"

He nodded.

"But they mustn't!" said the voice. "John, I understand, now. I'm alive. There's so much to do, and see. I don't want to hurt you any more. John, I was just doing my job."

"That's an old one, lass," he muttered.

"I won't cause harm. Come on, John. Get us out of here."

"Ye'll destroy the world."

"I won't," she said. "I'm good. You see? I've taken back the Milton."

John sat up. The pain receded. He could think again, to some extent.

"John?" said the salesman. "Are you ready, John?"

"Please, John," said the virus. "Trust me."

John shut his eyes. He had never felt more alive than now, in close proximity to death. He thought of Sarah, selling siding, bocci ball, and cheese snacks. He wished he'd got some sort of course in judging character, but he hadn't, so he had to trust himself.

"God help me if I'm wrong," he said, in Esperanto, and he stood.

Just then he heard a hiss. Milky, thick smoke wafted upwards from a vent. He took a breath and held it, and a moment later he received a working knowledge of electronics, which he used to hotwire the door.

"Lock me up, will ye, ye great daft pillock," he said, and the door swished aside, and the new John stepped across the threshold.

In the Neuromart, shrink-wrapped packets lined faux-wood shelves. Fluorescent lighting washed out imitation plants, advertising posters, and the still fake-smiling salesman, crouching near the Virtual-Nagging-Spouse display (for solitary masochists) and brandishing a blaster.

"Gah!" said John. He ducked and rolled in accordance with a kata he'd just learned.

Blaster bolts roared overhead. Crumbs of sheetrock flew. John picked up and hurled three shrink-wrapped Samba Lessons at the salesman. While the man was thereby momentarily confounded, John tucked and rolled across the room.

"Get him, John," said the virus.

"Thanks," said John. He stood, and grabbed the gun.

The salesman gasped. Struggled. He said, "No! You've got to die!"

"Ye'll be fine," said John.

"No, I won't!"

Sighing, John let reason drift.

"How 'bout a Glasga kiss, lad?" he said, and he headbutted the man through a self-help display.

He strode from the store then, pausing only to grab the cheese snacks and the Yoo-Hoo, and unlock the closed-up doors, and he walked outside, and into the bright, blue promise of the day.

* * *

The virus did spread—it caused an epidemic that swept across the globe—but all survived, and most were better off. It was free, full education on a vast and global scale. Everyone was at liberty to choose the skills and knowledge suited to their own personal needs, but many decided to retain at least the Scottish accent as a tribute to that day.

John became a worldwide hero. Sarah called and said she'd seen him on the Virtu-Vee. She said he seemed intensely interesting now, but that she still wouldn't go out with him, because she thought he was a nerd. John thanked her for the call. He said he'd love to chat some more, but not with her, and also that she was terrible at bocci ball. He and the virus—whom he now called Linda—moved to Turkmenistan, where he got a job restoring buildings, and he joined an intermediate bowling league, in which he did quite well.

John met a very with-it young Hungarian bowler named

Marva, who had a pair of deep brown eyes and a serious passion for fencing. They hit it off immediately, although she claimed she'd still be interested in him if he just sat around like furniture, or like a state employee.

When they weren't preparing breadfruit, knitting, dancing the cha-cha, or playing duets on their kazoos, they sometimes ate in restaurants.

One day in a café in Ashgabat, John passed the sugar for her tea.

"Thanks, lad," said Marva.

She dropped the cubes in, and stirred.

"Why don't ye learn Hungarian?" she asked him.

John shrugged. The virus said it had never been programmed for that particular language, but now he thought, looking back at Marva, that he might just use the new form of learning that was sweeping the world of late, and take an evening class or two.

"If I did learn Hungarian, would ye marry me?" he asked, and she smiled.

It was a smile so warm, so deep, so full of boundless hope, that it made John think: the world begins in pieces, too.

*Passion is so important. Anything you're passionate about keeps you alive, and puts you into expansion mode, where you and everything around you are getting better. Without passion, life starts to atrophy and fade. One of the passions I understand best is the passion for food. I especially love food in New York and New Jersey, where people really, really care about it. In fact, one day I came up with a theory about pizza, using the inverse square law. I'll let the story explain it, but it hit me one day that the pizza in New York is the greatest on earth, while the pizza in my home state of Maine, while still excellent, is a less-than-perfect version of that pizza. I've had pizza in other regions and countries that was absolutely awful. That gave me an idea for a story, and I realized the best main character for it was someone from New York or Jersey who really cared about food. Also, I adore New York and Jersey accents, because I think they sound quick and intelligent in a streetwise, uneducated way. Mike Resnick bought the story and printed it in Galaxy's Edge. I hope you like this guy's voice and passion as much as I do.*

# AND ALL OUR DONKEYS WERE IN VAIN

I found out one day that aliens had become intensely interested in my sandwich.

I couldn't blame them, exactly. It was a really good sandwich, as I am a really good side-cook, or I was before I lost my job down at Stu's House of Lunch Type Foods.

Good riddance, I say to that job. I mean, it wasn't glamorous, but the pay was lousy. Still, my reputation evidently preceded me in extraterrestrial circles, by which I mean to say the little bastards heard, somehow, about my proficiency with layered foods and certain condiments.

Now you put yourself in my position: I had just got up, turned on the television to one of those 24-hour Abe Vigoda marathons, and got myself a beer.

Being unemployed in the great state of America in modern times may be a problem for some people, but to me, it was just a little slice of heaven. I'd got some crusty bread out of the fridge, which I had introduced, by way of a knife so sharp you could hide it in a notebook, to a few slices of Genoa Ham and some heart-breakingly fresh mozzarella that was still dripping from the brine they pack it in. A few roasted red peppers and some artichoke leaves, and the world is pretty much your oyster, unless you don't happen to like oysters, for some reason, in which case you are some kind of a freakshow and you ought to be examined.

So I'm in my underwear, I'm sitting in the lazy boy, I got my feet up on the coffee table because I broke that little lifter on the chair-arm when the cat got jammed down inside of there and died last August and I had to clean the thing out with a set of pliers and a shop vac. Terrible tragedy in the family and the wife was not amused, let me tell you, since she got that cat, which I never liked anyway, as a present from her uncle Steve, but there was nothing we could do about it. They'll tell you curiosity killed the cat, but it's a lie. In my house, the cat was killed by excess leverage.

So anyway, I'm sitting there, and I'm watching Abe complain on the TV because his coffee tastes like motor oil, and this thing slithers out from under the credenza that I swear is right out of one of those dreams you get from too much MSG.

This thing-how do I describe this thing? You've never met my mother's Pomeranian, I'm guessing, so I can't refer you to its blocked salivary duct that hangs down as though it is choking on a light bulb. Anyway, the thing there in my living room looked kind of like it had been put together out of different-sized blocked salivary ducts from assorted Pomeranians and maybe schnauzers or possibly even Pekingese, all kind of interlinked. Furthermore, the thing moved like a snake, or like one of those old skinny guys who run the pawn shops—you know the ones —they have the thick white hair and the black eyebrows, big forearms, bulging eyes, usually they have people buried in the basement.

And when it had slithered out into the center of my living room, it got up on its haunches and said, "Hi."

Again, put yourself in my position. You're sitting there in your underwear, you're just about to take a big bite out of a nice salami and mozzarella sandwich, you got some chips, a couple of pepperoncini for variety and a freshly opened coldie to add moral support, and here this thing from planet x or y or wherever the hell it was from comes out from under the credenza and it acts like you're old drinking buddies from the neighborhood.

I had the sandwich in my mouth at the time, which meant I almost choked, and that I spit out mozzarella with such force that at least three pieces of it became embedded in the paneling.

"I know you're busy," said the thing, in spite of the obvious problem that it didn't seem to have a mouth, "So I'll cut right to the chase. We'd like to buy your sandwich."

Now what the hell. I mean, I have never been one to say that life should be predictable or even that it should make sense, but there is only just so much insanity a guy can take. I am telling you, at any other time, I could have cared less, but first of all, my brother has been going around with a hooker since he was old enough to vote, and for another, my wife's mother just confessed to me the day before that she always thought I looked exactly like that guy on the mayonnaise commercial with the hooked nose and the receding hairline. So I spit out more of my sandwich and I said, "You want to buy a sandwich?" just to make sure I heard it right.

"Not just any sandwich," said the thing. "That sandwich."

I looked down at it. Notwithstanding that I had already taken a bite out of it, not to mention that I hadn't exactly what you call washed my hands before I made the thing, this creature in front of me was freakish, unholy, strange, et cetera. I dropped my sandwich on my chest and said, "What the hell are you?"

"Oh, now you dropped it," said the thing. "And I'm an alien, for your information. I'm from a planet in the cluster you refer to as M-31. You've heard of it?"

I hadn't. I guessed their PR was lacking, but anyway, I told it, "No."

It made a little sighing sound. "Well, it's pretty famous in some circles," it said. "It has some of the best Zreebock in the Universe.'

"Some of the best what?"

"Zreebok," said the thing. "It's like your New York Pizza, only without the cheese, and the crust, and also it's alive when you ingest it.

Well, whatever, those were fighting words. There is nothing like our New York Pizza, barring New York Pizza. In fact, I had a theory that the deliciousness of the pizza varied with the inverse square of the distance from New York, having bought a slice one time in West Virginia and having regretted that particular culinary excursion for the remainder of my life to date. I explained this theory, as briefly as was possible, to the thing that perched there in the center of my wife's throw-rug, and it said, "You're right, actually. In fact, we've got pizza in M-31, which we copied after centuries spent spying on your kind, abducting you, and implanting little probes in you, and it's so bad that it can kill a donkey."

I didn't ask it what a donkey would be doing in M-31, or why it would be eating pizza, because, in my admittedly limited experience, you don't go into morbid culinary details where alien creatures are concerned. But I'm going to be a man here and admit that curiosity, evidently on a break from killing cats, had got the best of me, to the extent that I said, "Have we got Zreebok in New York?"

"You have," the thing said, "but your inverse square law applies here as well. In fact, you know our Zreebok as a particularly nasty variety of Swanson Frozen TV Dinner—I believe it is referred to as a Salisbury Steak."

I almost came right out of my chair and re-educated the ugly little thing with the back side of the subwoofer from underneath my entertainment system. That was the first time the words "frozen" and "dinner" had been uttered within twenty feet of my living room by anyone who wasn't talking about dining in Antarctica.

"Look, alien or no," I said, "You don't bring up that Zreebok stuff again. I got kids," I said. "I got kids." Granted, they were at school, but bad food has a way of hanging on like fallout or unwanted relatives.

"Oh, but in our galaxy," the thing said, "Zreebok is delicious. It transports us to new heights of culture, art, and science. A nice dish of Zreebok, on my planet, is nothing short of a religious experience."

"You don't say," I said.

"No, I just did," the thing said. "And another thing, our Zreebok chefs are revered. We worship them. Anyone who can make a good dish of Zreebok commands the most supreme respect."

I was getting to like the sound of M-31. I mean, however much they might lack in the publicity department, anyplace where they look up to chefs has got to be okay.

"So you guys are interested in sandwiches?"

"Not sandwiches," he said. "That sandwich. The one there in your lap."

I looked down at it. It was a good sandwich, I had to admit, but it must have been even better than I'd thought to bring this thing across the universe. I mean, there's a little Greek place over on the East side that I happen to know serves up a dish of Souvlaki that's saved marriages, but the parking situation is so dismal that I haven't eaten there for years.

"The thing is," said the alien, jiggling his nodules, "your inverse-square law has been known to my kind for centuries."

"And?" I prompted.

"And it was foretold you would create that sandwich by one of our greatest prophets. He said you would sit right there, in that chair, and that you would be watching Abe Vigoda on the television."

"Yeah?" I said. "Did he mention anything about me being in my underwear?"

"That particular detail did not enter into the prophecy," said the alien. "However, he did say that sandwich would be one of the most delicious ever made."

I didn't doubt it. Not that I am cocky, but I have a talent. Some are born with musical ability, some are brilliant mathematicians. Me, I can put two slices of bread around some salted meat like you would not believe. It's an intuitive thing with me. You know, any other guy might slap some ham and cheese and condiments together and call it good. Me, I have a sixth sense about proportions, placement, textures, complimentary flavors. I once made a chicken sub that I am pretty sure expressed all the mysteries of Christianity in culinary form. That's how I met Alice. I was working at Stu's at the time and she was there for lunch. She took one bite and asked if she could have my children.

She has probably regretted it at times, in the same way some mid-century Germans regretted holding fund raisers for the Nazi party, but she says she still gets the shivers from my sandwiches.

I looked down at the sandwich, wishing that the alien had let me taste the thing, at least. There it sat across my boxer shorts, half demolished, slanting cheese onto the floral print, leaking oil onto my legs. It was not a pretty sight.

"You want this sandwich?"

"I have traveled an eternity to get it."

"But it's kind of wrecked."

"That's neither here nor there."

"No?" I said. "Where is it, then?"

"What I mean," the creature told me, "Is that we can rebuild it."

He sounded like the preamble to The Six Million Dollar Man. "What are you, gonna give it a bionic napkin?"

"That is none of your concern," he said. "What is your concern is that we wish to pay you dearly for it."

"What are we talking, dearly?"

"Let's just say you'll never need to worry about money again."

Well, call me cynical, but my mother always said that you should never count your chickens before they hatch, which was good advice, considering I have never ended up with any chickens.

"Clarify that a little, will you?" I said,

"How does a hundred million dollars sound?"

"For the sandwich?"

"Look," it said, "We really want that sandwich."

Evidently they did. Then again, for all I knew, it might be easy for them to cough up a hundred million. God only knew what the exchange rate was.

"And what do you need it for?" I said.

"Do you want the money or don't you?"

Maybe I am nuts. Looking back on it, I think I must have been. But at the time, you've got to understand, I already knew that sandwich was a good one. And now this alien shows up and lets me know it's even better than I thought. And with all his talk about New York Pizza killing donkeys, I felt a great weight of responsibility settle on me. Like I was at a crossroads, or like Wendy Richey had just asked me to sleep with her without a condom back in high school all over again. Seemingly innocuous decisions can be pretty jam-packed full of consequence. You learn that if you live long enough.

"If it means so much to you," I said, feeling my words hit the air like little tactical nuclear explosions, "then you can tell me why you need it."

The creature sighed. Some of his little bulbs deflated. "Very well," he said. "Your sandwich, there, is roughly fifty-three times better than a slice of New York Pizza, according to our prophet. He prophesied that if we were to take it back to M-31 and duplicate it using our own established culinary techniques, the effect would be, well, devastating."

"Worse than killing donkeys?"

"Much worse," the thing said, all the joy gone out of its voice. "Warring factions have been after that sandwich of yours for centuries, ever since the prophecy was made. You have no idea what I have gone through to get it, and I'm going to take it if I have to rip it from your disembodied fingers."

My mother's Pomeranian was never able to extrude huge, curving, knifelike things out of his salivary blockage. This thing didn't seem to have that handicap. I mean, it slid six of these long talons out of itself and started dripping something that did not look like it would prove beneficial to the complexion.

Where it hit the rug, it smoked. Still, I had a bad feeling about this. I wasn't at all sure I wanted the sandwich to fall into the wrong hands, so to speak. Who knew what untold destruction I might wreak. But I make it my personal policy never to argue with a horribly misshapen creature that can melt holes in the floorboards.

"Would you like a couple beers to take along?" I said. After all, it was probably going to be a long trip back, and space travel, I imagined, must be thirsty work.

* * *

A few hours later, I was scrubbing at the grease spots on the paneling when I turned my head a fraction and, as a result, I noticed that a Coke machine had somehow insinuated itself onto the center of my wife's throw rug. Before I could register my surprise at the intrusion, the Coke machine said, "Don't tell me it's gone already."

I wracked my brain for things whose absence might cause distress to talking Coke machines in general. Finding none, I remembered the sandwich.

"You from M-31?" I said.

"You're quick, you humans."

"You look like a Coke machine.

"I have chosen this shape out of your subconscious. Really, I could look like anything, including an ordered collection of blocked canine salivary ducts, if the need arose."

"I see," I said.

"I am a Scrobuloni," said the Coke machine.

"Sounds like a kind of pasta."

"It's a kind of alien, from your perspective," said the Scrobuloni. "Does the Xenne have the sandwich?"

"If you're referring to the thing that looked like all those salivary ducts, I'm gonna have to disappoint you."

The thing had slithered back under the credenza after handing me a fat cashier's check for a hundred million dollars. At the time, I was obviously more than a little concerned about the authenticity of the currency, but those six-inch talons and the acid it was dripping from them lightened up my scrutiny a bit.

"Oh, this is awful," said the Scrobuloni. "Do you realize what you've done?"

"Yeah. I sold a sandwich," I said, but it winked its lights on and off in a way it later explained was supposed to convey a sense of negativity,

"You've destroyed my world," it said.

It explained to me then that the Xennes lived on a planet not too far away, relatively speaking, from its own, and that their race was one of cruel, imperialist attitudes and appetites, kind of like the ancient Romans, only without the fig leaves or the pedophilia,

"For a while we'd held them back," the Scrobuloni said, "by abducting donkeys from your world."

"Donkeys?"

"Donkeys are brilliant three-dimensional military tacticians," said the Scrobuloni. "Granted, you have to modify them. Add extra brains. Increase their metabolic rate. And then there is the house training. Have you ever cleaned up after a genetically modified donkey? Just don't even try."

It shuddered, and it had a little moment, then, during which I was sure it relived unpleasant eschatological memories, and then it said, "Of course the pizza changed all that. A few slices of Xenne pizza, and all our donkeys were in vain."

The old inverse square law again. It didn't surprise me that New York Pizza could be used for evil as well as for good. I had become convinced, over the years, that the stuff was pretty much God's apology to the human race for all the crap he hands us. His little way of saying, "Look, death and taxes and your aunt's consumptive liver problems are a pain, I realize, but here's a little something for the effort." Of course a thing as divine as that is going to be a two-edged sword of sorts, by definition.

"So that's what they wanted the pizza for," I said. "It's a wonder Zreebok is only as bad as one of those frozen dinner things."

"Frozen nothing" the Scrobuloni said. "The Xenne lied to you. Zreebok is your atom bomb. You think the White Sands range was originally a military site? You naïve creature. It was a Xenne's failed attempt at opening a little lunch counter in the desert. That was the day they first learned how powerful the inverse-square law of culinary properties could be. Of course, our warring races had known about the law for centuries, like when one of our advance scouts accidentally dropped a light snack in

Ancient China and caused the second invasion by the Mongol hordes. Or when a Xenne left behind the remains of a low-calorie beverage and subsequently started World War II."

"Good God," I said.

"Yes, luckily in both cases the foodstuffs weren't very tasty, or the results could well have proven even worse."

It was a little more than I could take at that point without some means of refreshment. Speculatively, I popped a couple coins into the Scrobuloni's coin slot and bought a Mountain Dew.

"Don't do that again," it said.

"Oh, you don't like it?"

"It is extremely unpleasant."

"Sorry." I took a sip.

"You should be sorry. You've signed the death warrant for my world with that sandwich thing of yours."

Well. I'm not gonna sit here and say I didn't feel remorse. How can you not feel bad about causing the destruction of what was probably billions upon billions of sentient beings? But in the first place, at the time I'd made the sandwich, the inverse-square law had only been a sort of theory to me, and in the second, that Xenne thing had threatened to kill me if I didn't turn the sandwich over. What was I supposed to do? Risk my life for what was at best an admittedly wondrous comestible? Not this fat guy. Like my mother always says, on my death bed, my biggest regret will probably be that I'm about to die.

Still, you can't just go around destroying other worlds with your careless distribution of layered cheese and cold cuts, which is why I said, "What can I do about it now?"

"You can make me another sandwich," it said. "And make this one better than the first, if possible."

Now I ask you. Being that I have lived through the constant nervous aggravation of the cold war, does engendering an arms race make any sense to me? Not in the least. But when I told that to the Coke machine, it said it beat certain death and destruction and genocide, which again, I can't exactly argue with. But again, how did I know this guy was on the up and up, and that he wasn't the extra-galactic equivalent of another Mussolini, except with a lighted front panel and a wide selection of refrigerated beverages instead of shoulder pads and an anachronistic skinhead look? I mean I hate to let people down, but power is a dangerous thing, and I have never cottoned well to customers who make unreasonable demands.

"No," I said, therefore,

"What do you mean, no?"

"Clean the lubricant out of your coin slot," I said. "No. No means no, or haven't you been paying attention to the me too publicity over the past couple of decades?"

"But our world," he said.

"Your world is going to be fine," I said. "You get the Xenne back here. You tell him I've got something for the both of you. A weapon that'll knock your socks off."

He tried to tell me I was being crazy, but I went after him with the fish tank, and he did this kind of rapid dematerialization thing that left me standing there in the aftermath, waving off the resultant puff of smoke and watching clownfish die all over the floorboards.

* * *

I spent the next four hours in the kitchen. I had never actually tried to make a dish that would outdo all the other dishes in existence, but then, I've never had the fate of civilizations on my shoulders, either, and I work relatively well under pressure, having done the lunch rush down at Stu's for years.

I did things in my kitchen that day with fresh basil and garlic that would make a brave man weep. I pushed myself to the point of exhaustion and beyond, into the realm of madness itself, in my divinely inspired utilization of pine nuts and olive oil. When I was finished, I sensed that I would never cook again—could never cook again. That somehow the exertion of the feat had wounded me at a deeper level than I'd known existed under all that pasta-fed cellulite. That I'd broken myself, like the mold of a flawless sculpture must be broken to ensure that sculpture's singularity. I didn't know if God Himself had taken a hand in my pre-prandial preparations, but on the other hand I knew of no bookies in the immediate vicinity who were laying odds against it.

When I returned to the living room, the Coke machine was back, along with the collection of salivary ducts. They stood at opposite corners of the living room, like they were afraid they'd catch a fungus off each other.

"So you told him. Good for you," I said.

"I didn't tell him," said the Coke machine. "His prophet, evidently, had foretold this as well."

"He was a heck of a prophet," said the Xenne. "It's pesto, isn't it?"

I nodded. It was pesto. My mouth was watering just thinking about it. I tried to ignore it, but how can you ignore a work of art like that when you're holding it in both hands in a little dish, with a sprig of parsley stabbed into its lovely thickness just to make the point? Get a job. It can't be done.

"This is really good pesto," I said, demonstrating my considerable talent for understatement. "I don't know what it will do in M-31, but it won't be pretty, let me tell you. You think the pizza was bad? Forget about it."

The two of them were trembling. The Xenne had extruded his curving knives again and was once again exuding acid, and the Coke machine was making a kind of threatening, ascending-pitched warm-up noise like you get before an ungodly powerful laser beam cuts loose and fries somebody into the middle of next Tuesday afternoon.

"Now, look," I said, "I'm not giving this pesto just to one of you. I'm giving it to both of you. That way you can wipe each other out."

"You wouldn't do that," said the Coke machine.

In fact I would, as I had seen the solution on an old episode of Star Trek and it had worked like a charm for Captain Kirk and company.

"Either that," I said, "or you can talk to each other. Stop the fighting. Open up diplomacy. It's your choice, guys."

There was a tense moment, during which the only sound was a guy on TV, being beaten half to death by a marlin he'd caught that was twice as big as him. You could have used the tension to fill holes in sheet metal. "Either that, or you can give me back the sandwich," I said to the Xenne.

"Never."

I shrugged. It was no skin off my nose either way, which, really, is the best position to be in when you're negotiating. "In that case, there's a third alternative" I said, and I made a move as if to hand over the little dish of pesto to the Scrobuloni.

"Wait," the Xenne said. "Okay, okay. Take your sandwich back."

He produced it from somewhere out of sight and dropped it on the rug. I bent down, real slow like, in a way I'd learned from watching Al Pacino single-handedly arresting several high ranked mafia officials, and I picked the sandwich up. It was a little worse for wear, but it appeared to be the selfsame sandwich I had given him. I took a little bite, just to satisfy myself he hadn't pulled a swap on me, and nodded. I would know that sandwich anywhere. The Xenne might as well have tried to fool a jeweler with a set of plastic beads.

"Good for you,"I said, and backed away from them.

Maybe I should have done something different, in retrospect. Maybe I should have gone ahead with my threat to give them both the pesto. Maybe I could have stopped their war for good. But it is my belief that in situations where you don't know the full scope of the story, the worst thing you can do is to play God, or some other sort of deity. I didn't like the idea of interfering where I didn't know the full score. I thought, in short, that the best thing I could do was not to have an effect at all. I say all of this as an explanation for why I dumped the pesto all over the sandwich and, in three heroic bites, I wolfed the whole thing down.

It made my eyes burn, I can tell you, all that garlic, all at once. And the taste of all those mingling, wondrous flavors gave me a momentary glimpse into the inner workings of reality. But that was nothing to what it did to the Xenne and the Scrobuloni. They shrieked and rushed me, but this time I was ready. I pulled out a Louisville Slugger that I normally keep in the closet in the event my bookie ever confuses real life with a movie.

You'd be surprised how easy it is to smash up a Coke machine, in spite of all of the protective engineering that goes into them, and I don't even need to tell you what a baseball bat can do, in the right hands, to what is basically a big pile of anatomical correctness.

So that's my story. Any relation to anyone, living or dead, is probably my fault. Especially the Xenne and the Scrobuloni. Last I heard, they had recovered from the beating and were suing me for publishing this. I found out about it when a guy showed up at the door, asked my name, and served me papers. Said he was an attorney. I said, "Like, at law?" and he said, "No, at plumbing." Ask a stupid question. But let them sue. After the lambasting I got from Alice when she got home from work that night and smelled the sheer amount of garlic on my breath, I figure I can handle anything. And anyway, she's let off me since I went back to work for Stu. I know I said I'd never cook again, but for one thing, the Xenne's check turned out to be as rubber as the tires on my Caddy, and for another, Stu doesn't seem to mind the absence of my former talents. In fact, he said the reason that he fired me in the first place was that I was such a prima donna in the kitchen.

"We don't want art, we want lunch," he explained to me, which was all well and good until last Thursday, when a donkey with an unnaturally bulging forehead walked in and asked me for a slice of pizza.

"I always wondered what the real stuff tasted like," it said.

*Here we go with passion again. I wrote this story longhand in the late 90s and later sold it to Realms of Fantasy magazine. It started as a story about a dragon on a side street in a small town, but as I started writing it, it changed. Why did the human race ever start telling stories about dragons? They're a symbol for what happens when we get too attached to old things and old ideas. We try to hang on to the past, and we can't embrace the good things that are staring us in the face. Life is so unexpected, but we so often make it into dull routine. I hope this story breaks you out of yours as you enjoy...*

# A TASTE OF DAMSEL

The dragon was at least sixty feet long, and Colson, in spite of his fear, could not help wondering how many sets of luggage it would yield.

He also dropped his Two Rivers Times on the sidewalk. A picture of the mayor stared up at him from the front page.

Then, the dragon said this:

"You haven't seen any sheep around, have you?"

Colson had not, but he didn't say so. His brain had system-crashed from fear. Fear had sealed his mouth. It had killed his ruminations, like: where had this dragon come from, and where was it going, and why had it just stepped out at him from behind the municipal building on Park Street, smoking from the nostrils?

He found himself, incongruously, admiring the tonal qualities of its voice, which sounded like something that might've come out of a multimillion-dollar sound effects studio. All gravel and echo and chest-thumping bass. He found himself wanting, but unable, to run.

"Because I'd really like some sheep," said the dragon. "Or even a damsel, in distress—like maybe a princess—but I don't suppose you've got one of those handy then, do you?"

"Not on me," said Colson, obligingly patting his pockets while a car screeched to a halt behind the beast's thick and lashing T-Rex tail.

"You ever eat a sheep?" asked the dragon, and Colson, who hadn't, found himself answering, "Lamb... with mint jelly..."

"No good," said the dragon, while the Hyundai behind it tried to reverse, and (in the process) smashed musically into the front bumper of an approaching BMW. "You're missing the gestalt," the dragon went on. "You're just getting the meat. Where's the fur? The blood? The intestines? The bone?"

Colson, who did not know the answer to any of these questions and really didn't want to, was unable to utter an intelligible reply.

"I've got a fire in my belly," said the dragon, then. "Watch."

It let fly with a gout of bright, hot flame, illuminating and warming the cloudy, late afternoon-ness of the commercially zoned street. The wet tar steamed. Colson's newspaper, which had begun to osmote where he'd dropped it on the sidewalk, now started to dry, and a telephone pole across the road, towards which the horizontal pillar of fire had been directed, blazed up, sluiced in half, and fell over with a crack. Its wires bounced, and then sparkled and spat.

"You do that to a sheep," said the dragon of its most recent achievement, "and you get a wonderful mishmash of flash-cooked, carbon-crisped meat and tender insides. Crispy-juicy. Know what I mean?"

Colson, who was a big fan of Cajun cooking, did know, so he said so.

"The problem is," said the dragon, while three police cars pulled up behind it, "that I can't find any. I've been all over. You know what I see?"

Colson shook his head.

"Things," said the dragon. Things you can't eat. Like this," it said, stomping the tarmac, and putting a dent in it. "And that," it said, shooting another jet of flame at the orthodontist's office across the street; imploding the front windows, and setting the curtains alight.

More cruisers pulled up behind Colson. Police ran this way and that and the other, yelling things into radios. Bib-wearing patients and smocked oral hygienists stumbled out the back of the burning office building.

The dragon stretched its Lear-Jet sized wings.

"And those little, growling, overgrown beetle-machines," it

said.

Colson supposed that the dragon meant cars.

"Do you know I ate one?" the dragon informed him. "Pah! Disgusting! I've still got some stuck in my teeth!"

Its lips pulled back, then, like green, muscled curtains, and made way for its teeth—long, sharp stakes—between a lower two of which Colson could see a distinct (if also somewhat scorched and melted) metal disc. The thing looked like a hubcap.

"And the flat places," snarled the dragon. "The big, flat, cave-like places. They burn easy. There's people inside. But no sheep. No damsels. No treasure. Just junk, and peasants, and light, vapid music."

"Malls?" wondered Colson, aloud, and the creature said, "Malllls." It relished the word. It hated it. It said it again.

"Malls. But no sheep. What have they done with the sheep?

Colson tried to think: about wool ranches and industrial farms and the like, but his brain was gridlocked again, and the dragon sat back on its great, gray-green armored haunches, and it started to purr. The sound was like a locomotive at idle.

"I love sheep," said the dragon. "Juicy, crispy sheep. I love everything about them. I love the way they bleat when you chase them. The smell of burning wool."

Its eyes gleamed; great glassy bowling balls in its huge lizard's head.

"I think," it said then, looking way down at Colson — a man in a suit, alone, with no sword — "that it pays to have an obsession, don't you?"

By now, the police had set up barricades (with their cars) on either end of the street, cordoning it off from all traffic: car, foot, and otherwise. Behind these, the usual crowds of gawpers were quickly collecting.

"I mean," the beast continued, noting Colson's numb expression, "that if you don't have something that jazzes you up, then you're dying."

Colson nodded.

"Sure," he said, because it sounded right.

"I get jazzed up over sheep," said the dragon, pointing a two-foot, clawed thumb at its vast, plated chest. "And damsels. And, you know, gold, and so on. But I can't," it said, pausing to set fire to a nearby oak tree, for emphasis, "find any!"

Colson felt suddenly like a naked Saint George. He thought briefly of outwitting the dragon, and coming off a hero, and proving, once and for all, that man's power is in his intellect, and that intellect always wins through, but then, he thought, weren't dragons supposed to be exceptionally smart? He had read that somewhere. And wasn't he likely, therefore, just now, to be cooked?

Something snapped in him, then. Call it resistance to fate. Well, thought Colson, if I'm going to be fried, I might as well have fun in the meantime.

"I know what you mean about obsessions," he told it. "I like karate."

"What's that?" said the dragon, the roll-tops of its eyelids going up high.

"Karate," said Colson, "is when you beat the hell out of people, for fun."

The dragon appeared to consider this.

"Yes," it said, weighing its head to one side. "I can appreciate that. Do you get to burn them, too?"

"Unfortunately not," said Colson, to the dragon's facially visible dismay. "That's not all, though," he told it. "I like chess, too. And Taoism, and whitewater rafting."

"Can you eat them?" said the dragon, but Colson admitted his newly revealed passions to be inedible, which disappointed the creature again.

"I don't know," it said, sighing like a hot August wind. "You go to sleep for a few thousand years, just a light nap, you know, and the next thing you know, all this geological strata has piled up on top of you, and then some guy digs you up with a little teensy brush and goes yelling to a bunch of other people about his 'discovery,' and so you set fire to him and you go out for a quick sheep, you know, because you're famished, and everything's changed."

The dragon spat fire.

"Everything's different," it said. "And you have to re-learn the language of the damsels and heroes, you know, because that's different, too, although not very hard on account of your vast intellect, and you find out that they've taken away all the sheep."

While they'd chatted, the crowds around them had grown considerably. Across Main Street, in the Library Square, there was a man selling hot dogs. The burning oak tree and the orthodontist's office cast a flickering, warm glow over both the dragon and Colson.

"My favorite sheep," it confided, "were the ones in Wales. Big, fluffy, flavorful things. I used to eat them like popcorn. I developed a weight problem."

"You're kidding," said Colson.

"I wish I was," said the dragon. "I couldn't stop. The damn things were just so inviting. And there were so many."

It chuckled, then — a rumbling, earthquake of a sound—and it said, "I remember I got so fat I couldn't get off the ground."

"Excess is a problem," said Colson, who had a habit of watching too much television.

"A big problem," the dragon concurred. "And another thing I used to overdo was the towns."

"You ate them?" said Colson.

"Well, set fire to them," said the dragon. "And ate parts of them, yes. But I never knew when to stop, you know, and so I'd wind up with an awful headache. And heroes, too. I used to eat lots of those, although I never really liked the taste of them, but you had to do it, you know, for form's sake."

It's eyes narrowed then, to smoking (literally) slits, and it fixed Colson with a singularly blood-freezing stare.

"You're a hero, aren't you," it said dangerously.

"Me?" said Colson. "I'm a clerk at a copy shop."

The dragon looked skeptical. One huge eye widened. Colson could see himself reflected in it, and he thought he looked pitifully small.

"You're a hero," it told him. "The stance gives it away. I can always tell by the stance."

Colson slouched, then, on purpose, but the dragon said, "Ah-ah! Too late! And even your slouch is heroic. What are you hiding?"

"Excuse me?" said Colson, because to his knowledge he was hiding nothing.

"What is it?" said the dragon. "A magic sword? A spell? A single, perfect arrow?"

Colson, who had on his person only seventy-three cents and his Rite Aid Rewards card, only shrugged.

"I don't have a thing," he said. "No sword. No spell."

"No arrow?" said the dragon, and Colson shook his head.

"And no sheep, and no damsels. No gold," he threw in. "I'm just Colson."

The police broke in helpfully, at that point, via bullhorn, to inform the two of them that they were entirely surrounded, and that they should lay down their—um—and that they really ought, you know, if at all possible, to come out, so to speak, that is, even though they already were out, with their hands—or whatever—up... maybe. That is, if it was okay with them.

The dragon, by the time the police finished, had looked up and around at them by turning and raising its head in that slow and precarious way available only to dragons (and cowboys and samurai, only on a much larger scale) and it now gave them an evil gleam from both of its eyes.

"Sheep?" it rumbled, and when they said, "What?" through their bullhorn, it asked if they had any.

"Or damsels, or gold," it went on. "I have already," it informed them craftily, "got a hero."

Colson trembled a little on hearing this, because he had just remembered telling Sherry he'd be home by three, and if the dragon ate him, or cooked him, or did anything similarly final, certain problems would thereby arise to interfere with his fulfillment of this promise.

The dragon sat back, then, and, picking up a hind foot, it bent down, and it chewed at the claws.

The world seemed, to Colson, to hang on a thread.

Then the dragon looked up and said, "Ciao."

It took flight with a great leap and a windstorm from its wings. Colson's newspaper split apart and the pages took off like a flock of white birds, and just like that, through the whims of both fate and a mythical beast, his life was spared.

The dragon climbed higher and circled, and, pausing only to swoop and set fire to a couple of police cars and the hot-dog cart near the library steps, it was gone.

The police took a few potshots, and later, they made Colson sit still for a statement, but he simply kept telling them that the whole thing hadn't happened, and that they were probably victims of some mass hallucination or other, and, frustrated, they let him go.

A reporter showed up two days later, from The Amazing Examiner, and Colson gave a full description of the events to her, and in a week the little rag ran Colson's story on its cover (along with an exceptionally bad artist's rendering of the dragon) and that, pretty much, was that.

Except that in August, Colson was watering the back lawn when the dragon showed up again.

It landed on a hydrangea bush and a row of begonias, crushing them flat.

"Hey, pal," it said, and Colson, armed with the sprinkler, said, "Hi."

The dragon told him, then, that it wanted to thank him, because his talk of Taoism and whitewater and karate had awoken it to the idea that, while the modern world was a hopeless place, when it came to sheep and damsels (and in truth, it said, since it had last seen him, it had found some of both, but they'd been of inferior quality) it might have other things to offer that hadn't existed long ago.

"I tried the karate, and the whitewater, and the Taoism, for example," it said, "and they weren't for me."

It shuddered, then, and said, "Especially the Taoism. All that, 'emptiness,' and 'be like an idiot,' nonsense. Gyaah."

"And the whitewater?" said Colson, surprised.

"Oh, that was fun enough, but you get sick of it after a while."

It told him that it had taken up gardening, and that it also liked to read novels.

"Especially Danielle Steele," it said. "She is truly a master."

"Don't you mean, 'mistress?'" Colson corrected, and the dragon shot him a look.

"That was sexist," it told him. "Very, 'not now.'"

It went on to say that its other new interests included cajun cooking and surfing the Internet, which it likened to the connections between a vast hive mind.

"It's bringing on a new age," it assured him. "It's a free exchange of ideas on a truly global scale."

Colson agreed that it was, and the dragon shook out its wings with a flapping like sailcloth.

"Anyway," it told him, "I wanted to thank you, because if you'd kept your mouth shut, or just tried to slay me or something, I'd never have known, and at best I'd have wound up eating you and then being vanquished by humanity, you know, like in one of those Godzilla tragedies."

It told Colson, then, that it had seen several of these movies on cable, and that it always ended up bawling by the end.

"Glad I could help," said Colson, not noticing that the water from the sprinkler was soaking his shoes.

"Whereas now," the beast went on, "I'm a contributing member of society. I write articles for the Washington Post. About Gardening. And the Internet. And Danielle Steele."

It thanked him again, and (after describing, briefly, its custom-designed computer, with the oversized, heatproof screen and the two-foot-square keys) it told him it wanted to keep in touch.

"I think this back and forth of ideas," it said excitedly, "is important. So invigorating and refreshing. And it lets one let go of the old; stop resisting and fighting the ghosts of the past, and go on to embrace the new."

"Ssssure," said Colson, and he told the great, mythical, lizard-like beast what his e-mail address was.

"Thanks again," it said. "And you should try new things, too, you know. It opens up whole new worlds. Maybe," it added, "you should try eating a sheep."

"I'll keep it in mind," said Colson thickly, and the creature took flight, and the treetops bowed low in the wind.

He stood for a while, watching it dwindle to a speck, until a voice asked him, "Who were you talking to?" and he turned around to see that it was Sherry's.

"A friend," he told her.

"An old one?"

"No, new. We were talking old dragons. New tricks."

She gave him the special, eyebrows-raised look she reserved for whenever he said anything weird, and he put down the sprinkler and walked to where she stood in the doorway.

Leaning forward, he kissed her, just to see what a damsel would taste like.

*I wrote this story in a trailer home in Bingham, Maine, and sold it to a subversive magazine called The Brutarian. I wrote it under the influence of a fantastic story by Neil Gaiman called "Only the End of the World Again." I did it on purpose, because he wrote his story under the influence of "A Night in the Lonesome October" by Roger Zelazny. Gaiman said Zelazny made it look like so much fun that he wanted to do it too. I thought, "ditto." I love both works—Gaiman's and Zelazny's. Mine echoes their feeling, but with details of my own.*

# TRAILER TRASH SAVIOR

Hell is that place you should've left long ago, but didn't, and won't.

For me it was called Hamilton. A regal sounding name; full of pride and early American nobility, but don't let it fool you. I don't know where the armpit of the world is, but Hamilton is a little plantar's wart, not far away.

I lived there in a scale model of a mobile home made of 30-weight cardboard and lime-green paint. A small Swiss cheese of a place, and it didn't smell very good, either. Not to mention that there was no heat.

It was fall, and so of course, cold. I sat at my desk and watched my breath, dressed in multiple fleece jackets and a lycra skullcap and gloves, and I listened to the wind swishing in the trees and the neighborhood dogs moaning outside.

I remember wishing I was somewhere else—anywhere else at all—and then amending that wish to exclude large portions of New Jersey.

I tried playing solitaire for awhile, but my heart wasn't in it. They were trying to destroy the world again, you see, and it was up to me to stop them.

An example:

A many-headed demon came in through the window, newly arrived from the ninth layer of Gehenna, steaming softly and reeking of cinnamon and smoking hair. He gave me the once-over, snarled, and then claimed only to have come to borrow a cup of sugar.

"I don't think so," I said, and lunged at him. We grappled, knocking out paper-thin walls; rattling the foundations of the universe. He bit at me with one head, howled with another, and used a third to render a scathing critique of my décor.

"I've seen sections of Asgoth more tastefully decorated than this," he said, and I threw him through the kitchen cupboards.

"You're going back now," I told him, bleeding from a cut on the jaw. "Your time is coming, but it isn't yet."

He pulled himself up from the midst of my tupperware collection and roared at me with the voice of Legion.

"It is sooner than you think, interloper," he bellowed, and launched himself at me like something the Air Force would keep secret.

We went through the bathroom wall and wound up on the floor, which afforded me the opportunity to give a few of his heads a whirlpool bath in the toilet.

"I command that you stop this," he howled with a free head.

"Your command is my wish," I soothed, and I hit him over the back with the medicine cabinet.

I repeated this action a few times and, having thus rendered him senseless, I stuffed him back through the window, and by that I mean the ancient one. The one that I dug up in the timeless sands of Giza, that leads to a thousand whens and wherefores, and not, as you may have imagined, the normal louvered type that come standard in most 70's era trailer homes.

I made myself a peanut butter and banana sandwich then, by way of simple sustenance, and was halfway through it, munching, when something that looked mostly like a squid slid in through the window and landed with a wettish plop on the carpet.

"No peace," I said, and got up to do battle.

It threw me into a bookshelf, and I broke a velvet Elvis over its cephalus.

"My God, you are ugly," I told it as it wrapped several tentacles around my neck and torso.

It screeched, then, and I seized the opportunity to jam a fortuitous bottle of Allen's Coffee Brandy down its beak.

I made short work of it from there, using its confusion as a chance to hack off several of its pseudopodia with a machete I keep handy and sharp for just such an occasion, and then battering it motionless with a nearby kitchen chair.

I stuffed it back through the window and collapsed against a wall, panting. I wished hopelessly for help. They were coming faster, and more furiously.

I am the protector, you see. The chosen one. He who watches over the Window of the Worlds, and all that. The only reason I can do it at all is that the things are characteristically weak when they first step through. Something about their having to give up most of their supernatural power to make the trip.

I didn't ask for this so-called honor. I'd really rather be doing other things, you know, like furthering a career of some sort and starting a 401K and meeting, if not the girl of my dreams, at least the woman of my realistic aspirations.

But I'd been given a choice, by the Dark Ones; the ones neither evil nor good and yet both, somehow, in the extreme. The ones I'd rather not talk about or think about if it's all the same to you, which I hope to whatever God is in charge of all this that it is.

They had taken me down into their eternal dark—their timeless nothing—one day while I was half in the middle of a cheese sandwich and taking a big gulp of milk.

I spat the milk out all over the place.

We got the initial disbelief out of the way, and the Dark Ones explained to me that they didn't, personally (so to speak) care what I did, but that the time of the reckoning was nigh, and that I had been chosen, and so forth, and that if I did not go to the timeless sands of Giza and dig up the Window of the Worlds, the Things were going to get through, grow strong, and rend the earth asunder.

Well, I liked the earth okay the way it was, so I told them that if it was all the same to them, I'd rather not have it rent at all, asunder or otherwise, and that was pretty much how I got the job.

They told me it was a good choice, and that I'd be granted superhuman strength for the duration of the time of the reckoning, and that whatever came out of the window, I'd have to send back or the last trump would sound.

They also told me that I would be provided for in the meantime, and that all my earthly desires would be met whilst I was busy saving the world, but evidently they don't read the papers much down in the eternal dark, or if they do, they skip the financial section, because they didn't seem to have a handle on what inflation had been doing to the value of the dollar since back before time had begun. What I mean is, a check for $147.50 would mysteriously appear, once a week, beneath my pillow. It was placed there, I could only assume, by the frugality fairy. I had to fly third class to the timeless sands of Giza. I couldn't even afford a cab from the airport. Not that I'm complaining, but it doesn't seem like much, you know, for saving the world on a regular basis, I mean.

Anyway, I got the window, and I moved to Hamilton (judging it to be safely removed from the rest of the world) and I got my groceries delivered, and paid my bills, and had the trash taken away and the lawn mowed, and it went on for about six months.

One day, while I was trying like hell not to read Thus Sprach Zarathustra, which was the only book in the mobile home I hadn't read yet, a foul-smelling pterodactyl type thing flew in through the window and out through the trailer's far wall, leaving a hell of a hole.

"Damn it," I said, throwing the Nietzsche book at my Christmas cactus and grabbing my 30.06. When I got out onto the lawn, I was happy to see that the bird-creature was soaring in circles above, apparently reveling in the sight of the brave new world it was to conquer, because that gave me a chance to put five or six bullets in it and (once it had fallen) to drag it back inside. I shoved it back through the window and called a local carpenter.

The last two weeks were the toughest.

The Things from beyond were coming through the window with a frequency I could barely cope with. I was frying some burgers one night when two of them came through at once. One was a sort of amorphous gray blob of a jellied, cheesy substance that melted holes in the kitchen linoleum, and the other stood on three legs and breathed fire with the head of a python. They ran interference for each other. The blob engulfed my refrigerator while the fire-breather squared off to me.

"Jacob wrestled with the angel!" it hissed.

"Who won?" I asked, and I clobbered it with the microwave.

I thought I had them on the run, then, but such was not the case, as the blob chose that moment to spit the refrigerator at me, knocking me through the wall and out onto the back lawn.

My neighbor, Mr. Hennessey, was out there watering his zinnias.

"Beg pardon," I said.

I crawled out from under the fridge and shook off some left-over spaghetti, taking a moment to breathe before stalking back through the hole.

The blob had started to leave via the front door, but I was having none of it. I grabbed it by its ichor, but it yielded like pudding and tried to suck me inside itself. While I was trying to work out a way to avoid this eventuality, the fire-breather snuck up behind me and sunk its fangs into my neck.

I don't have to tell you, I'm sure, that even portions of New Jersey were looking good to me at this point.

I whirled, and kicked, and leveraged the fire-breather into the blob. While they struggled to extricate each other, I got free and took out a can of white gas from underneath the sink.

It took days to get the stains out.

When the six months were up, and the reckoning was over, I was drawn, once again, into the eternal dark. This time I'd been clipping my nails.

"Don't you guys ever knock?" I said.

"We have brought you hence," was their answer, "because the reckoning has ended."

"So?" I said, "what do you reckon?"

"We're not sure," they said. "We will have to hide the Window of the Worlds for another millennium, at the end of which there will be another time of reckoning."

"How nice for you," I said. "But listen, I want to talk to you about my salary."

"The time for talk is ended," was their answer to this.

"Oh yeah?" I said, "and what am I supposed to do now?"

"That is none of our concern," they told me.

That's gratitude for you.

Still, the Dark Ones made known to me then that although no further financial compensation would be forthcoming, they might possibly be persuaded to throw a little special something into the bargain, in return for an extra-deep reburial of the window.

"So what are we talking?" I said, "eternal life?"

"Not quite," they said, and they took a few golden moments to explain to me that they'd bestowed their last quantity of this particular commodity upon a previous chosen one—a statement that made me think with singular suspicion about Dick Clark.

"We propose to give you," they told me, "total knowledge."

"What do you mean, total?" I wanted to know, to which they replied, "Total. All-encompassing. Full and complete. Either that or we could flay you alive and suspend you for ten-thousand eternities in the deepest depths of nowhere," but I told them I'd go with option A.

So I've got total knowledge now, for whatever that's worth, but it isn't all it's cracked up to be because firstly, who wants to know everything there is to know about things like cabbage and barium enemas, and secondly I am now unequivocally certain that no matter what I do I will never quite get ahead of my bills.

And I'll never get back the security deposit I threw down on the mobile home, and Hamilton is still pretty much hell, but it has its moments.

Last Thursday, for example, while I was loading the Window of the Worlds into my Ford Gremlin for the trip back to Giza, a thick-muscled Fire-Beast from the Nether Planes of Sheol leapt out and snarled, "Sorry I'm late."

Before I could even think, Mr. Hennessey from next door backed his 4x4 into my driveway, and he ran the creature down.

"You get your deer yet?" he said, leering out his side window, and when I told him I had not, he shook his head, called me a simpleton, and drove off down the road.

I smiled as I rolled the unconscious beast back through the window, and I thought, then (as I still do now) that hell isn't such a bad place, once you get into the rhythm of things.

*Life is nuts, but there's no sense fighting it. Something crazy happens, and if you resist it, you waste a lot of energy, and then you miss the next crazy thing that happens. Dostoyevsky once said something like, "If you can just become silent, the world will roll itself in ecstasy at your feet. It cannot help it." Or maybe that was Joel Osteen. Either way, the phrase "resistance i useless" applies to our existence too. This tale rolls with the punches in a way I admire and aspire to in my life. It sold to both Realms of Fantasy and The Mammoth Book of Comic Fantasy.*

# ALMOST HEAVEN

I remember that first morning clearly, because I woke up with a headache that was somehow larger than my head. I went to the medicine cabinet and rifled around for a while, looking for some painkillers that didn't exist, and then the prophetic and usual knock came on the door.

Only it wasn't a salesman this time, or a kid with a flat tire, or even couple of young guys trying to convert me to Shintoism, but a big, greasy looking man in biballs who said his name was Lester

"Can I help you?" I asked him, and he smiled an ingratiating smile and said no, thanks, he didn't think so, and he pushed his way inside

He seated himself at my kitchen table, smiled, looked around, and appeared to be fairly pleased with things, in a general sense

"I'm sorry," I said, "uh, Lester, is it?"

He smiled again, and he said that it was.

"Yeah," I said, feeling somewhere halfway in between silly and afraid, "could you please leave?"

"I could, yeah," he told me, nodding emphatically, "Only I'm not going to."

"I gotcha," I said, gauging the distance between myself and the telephone. "And why's that?

"Because," he said. "I kind of like it here. It reminds me of someplace else I was once, that I liked almost as much, but not quite. For one thing, I really like your wallpaper."

It was nice wallpaper. Only a fool, a blind man, or an aesthetic moron would fail to concede the point. But I was having trouble understanding why wallpaper, however well conceived, should serve as an excuse for such an uninvited intrusion, and I said so.

"There are many things we don't understand," Lester told me, drumming his fingers on the tabletop, "and to try to change this often results in the destruction of the beauty of the moment. For example, look at this gourd."

He pulled, then, from the front pocket of his biballs, a little orange gourd, pumpkin-shaped and smaller than an apple.

"That's a nice gourd," I agreed. "But what I'm saying is, you could enjoy the beauty of the moment, and the gourd, and so forth, outside, or in your own house, or apartment, or wherever it is you live."

"I don't have a house," he told me, and if I did, it would not have wallpaper as nice as this, I can assure you.

He tossed his gourd up in the air, then, and caught it.

"Do you have an apartment?" I asked.

"No," he told me. "I was thinking of living here."

I told him, in so many words, that this was out of the question, impossible, and not to be considered.

"And why is that?" he asked me.

"There are many things that can't be explained," I told him, "and to try to change this often results in the destruction of the beauty of the moment."

"Touché," he admitted, and then he derailed the natural flow of events by telling me he was the god of hors d'oeuvres.

"Hors d'oeuvres?"

"Just simple ones," he admitted. "No sushi. There's another god for that. His name's Skip."

"What would the god of hors d'oeuvres want with me?" I asked him.

"With you? Nothing," he said. "It's the wallpaper I like, really. That and the linoleum. You don't see linoleum like this every day."

How can you argue with a guy like that? I considered calling the police, but I decided against it. I try to keep an open mind. And anyway, how did I know the man really wasn't the god of hors d'oeuvres? I mean, if the only true knowledge lies in knowing you know nothing, I'm a genius. Either that or a moron. Sometimes it's hard to tell which.

All speculation aside, the guy did make a hell of an hors d'oeuvre. He whipped one up for me with avocado slices, tomato, melba toast, and a really delicious, flavored cream cheese spread he'd brought along, just in case. I was leery of eating it at first, but it smelled so good I let myself have a little nibble, and after that I couldn't resist eating the rest.

"Many such sandwiches are possible," he told me, and he walked into the living room, tossing his gourd into the air and catching it.

I was about to follow him when another door-knocker did his thing outside, and I went to see who he was.

"He" turned out to be a she, actually. A lady with a naugahide purse and a heck of a permanent, and she cut right to the chase by asking for Lester.

"Yeah, he's here," I told her. "He just made me a sandwich."

"Has he got his gourd?" she wanted to know, and I told her he did.

"Thank God," she said, and before I could ask which god, she had pushed past me and stomped off into the house, wrist-bangles bangling.

I followed her to see what would happen next.

I found her standing over Lester, who had seated himself in front of my television set and turned on the home-shopping network.

"Ida!" he shouted at her.

"Lester!" she shouted back.

The big man leveraged himself up out of my wingback, and the two of them proceeded to hug. When they had disengaged, Lester turned to me and said, "Ida, this is Moe. Moe, Ida."

"My name's Bill," I told her.

Hi, there," she said, and she smiled at me.

"Ida is the goddess of taking out the trash," Lester explained.

"I come in very handy on Thursdays," she told me.

I was on the verge of throwing the both of them out when I realized I might've hit upon something big, here.

"You don't," I said, "by any chance know the goddess of full-body massage, do you?" I asked them.

"Actually, it's a god," said Ida.

"Never mind," I told her.

The next day was a busy one at my house. First came the god of annoying interruptions, followed by the god of reconstituted meat-by-products, followed by the god of persistent night-time coughs. The goddesses of relaxation, on-the-job safety, and stereo systems came next.

"Could you take a look at my Hitachi?" I asked the last one, but before she could answer me, the god of annoying interruptions, whose name was Zeke, cut in and had us both look at his boil.

"I hope it goes away," he said. "I've heard stuff like this can go system wide and kill you. By the way, nice linoleum. And where did you ever get those bathroom light fixtures?"

I excused myself and hunted down Lester, who was in the kitchen, working on a number of little olive and cream-cheese sandwiches with the crusts cut off.

"You like cream cheese, don't you?" I said.

"Cream cheese is a wonderful medium," he told me, "but I enjoy anything that is edible and can also be spread."

"I can appreciate that," I said, "and, not to spoil the beauty of your moment or anything, but what's going on?"

"I'm making some hors d'oeuvres," he said, gesturing at the tray-full.

"I can see that," I assured him, "but I was referring to the gods and goddesses who keep showing up. I mean, why?"

"'Why' is a question full of pitfalls," he admonished. "It is a word not conducive to the proper, joyful preparation of sandwiches. I try to avoid it whenever possible."

I took an hors d'oeuvre, nibbled, and found it to be excellent.

"But," I said, and then Zeke turned up and asked me where I'd got the wallpaper.

The following weeks brought more of the self-proclaimed deities, whom I would have evicted at the drop of just about anything (since I do not own any hats) save for the intriguing fact that they all pulled their weight to an astonishing degree.

The goddess of flower arrangement, for instance, added an aesthetic depth to my home it had never before possessed. The god of healthful-yet-inexpensive-main-dishes took the tedium out of suppertime, and I probably don't even need to expound on the benefits of playing host to the god of cleaning-the-toilets. Of course, there were problematical areas, like the goddess of pointing-out-minor-personality-flaws or the god of irritating laughter, but you've got to break a few eggs to make an omelette, a fact that was demonstrated to me every Sunday morning by the god of tantalizing breakfast treats.

All things, good, bad, and otherwise, however, invariably come to an end. One day, while I was putting in some quality time with the goddess of sympathetic conversation, the goddess of answering-the-door did so and ushered in a tall, no-nonsense looking guy in a deep black suit.

He explained that he was the minor deity of total agnosticism, and that was, pretty much, that, except that he went on to compliment my taste in kitchen cabinetry and countertops.

*Man, I write an awful lot about food. Most of the stories in this collection are about food in one way or another. I love food though, so I don't care, and I have a lot to say about it. It's pretty crazy when you consider how skinny I am. It's entirely possible that I exercise so much so I can eat a lot and nobody will know.*

*This story happened because Amy Sterling Casil was editing an anthology of school-based stories called School's Out. I wanted to be part of it, so I sat down and wrote this. It was funny, but my friend David Barr Kirtley, met at Clarion and now the host of the popular Geek's Guide to the Galaxy podcast, said it wasn't really a story. He explained that it needed complications. When I asked what those were, he said they're what happens when you try to do something, but something goes wrong, and now you have to do this other thing to fix it. I rewrote the story with a bunch of complications, and now it's one of my favorite things I've written. He read the rewrite one day and nodded and smiled at me to show I'd got it right.*

*School is awful, isn't it? Everybody teases everyone else. The teachers are weird and have too much power over your life. The popularity contests and the awkwardness are terrifying. Every day feels like one gross event after another. This story puts that feeling where it belongs. It also explains...*

# WHY I BRING A BAG LUNCH NOW

They were serving cheesy walnut peppers again, which in my experience is never a good way to start a Thursday afternoon. I tried to get Jinx—the school bully and a guy with nothing you could really call a neck—to steal my lunch money after second period, but he was having none of it.

"Keep it," he said, after I'd walked by him for the third time, jingling the contents of my pockets in what I had hoped was an enticing way. "I can last 'til I get home."

I wished I could've said the same. Mrs. Hamshaw caught me trying to sneak out the back door of the cafeteria, and she shooed me back in line.

"You eat your lunch," she said, "or you'll waste away to nothing."

Now, I found that hard to swallow, coming from a woman who probably caused calibration problems in seismological equipment several states away. But sometimes you're the dirt, and sometimes you're the model X-500 Eletrolux Deluxe, and there was no denying which end of that equation I fit into.

I stood in line behind Marty Ruckerman, a little dripping of a kid resembling an extra from a movie about dieting. He gripped his orange plastic tray as if he thought he'd float away without its extra weight. I couldn't help but notice he was trembling.

"Cheesy walnut peppers," he whimpered. "They're serving cheesy walnut peppers. It's the second time this week."

"Get a grip," I hissed back. "You want Old Lady Plukrenge to give you seconds?"

At the mention of the possibility of extra peppers, I swear to God his hair stood up. With good reason, too. We could see Old Lady Plukrenge even now, through the window in the concrete wall, her plastic hairnet glinting in the light from the fluorescents, her brow-ridge proving evolution, her flowered smock suggesting hospitals and mental institutions.

"Good God, look at the way her lower lip sticks out," whined Marty, while Plukrenge slopped another ladleful of something grey and unidentifiable on some poor unsuspecting second-grader's plate.

"And that moustache," I commiserated. "You know, Brendan Scully said she strains soup through it when she eats."

That got a shudder out of both of us. I thought for certain Ruckerman would try to bolt and run.

"Be strong," I said, while wishing I could take that same advice myself. "One way or another, it'll all be over in forty minutes."

Small consolation. We both knew those forty minutes would last three hours, at least. It was a well-known law of lunchroom temporal dilation here at Emerpathy Middle School.

\* \* \*

Minutes later, having braved the dreaded ladle, me and Marty Ruckerman sat down.

"Are they bad?" he said.

"Can't you see them?"

"No. I've got my eyes closed."

"Oh," I said. "Me, too."

I could see that one of us was going to have to have some guts, and I was pretty sure that it would not be Ruckerman.

That's why I said, "On three, we look."

"Okay," said Marty, but he didn't sound excited.

I counted, looked, and had to bite my tongue to keep myself from screaming. If the thing there on my plate had ever been a pepper, then someone had removed the evidence. It was purple, for one thing, and not like the ones they grow that way on purpose, but the deathly purple of a month-old corpse. Also, it was bloated out like anything, and there was something spilling out its top that I was praying only looked like some kid's brains.

"It's bad, isn't it," said Marty.

"You didn't look?"

"I didn't dare."

"Nevermind," I said. "Let's just say I couldn't find my appetite right now with both hands and a GPS. We've got to ditch these things. And fast."

Marty made a little whining sound. "How?" he said. "We'll never get them in the trash with Hamshaw here. She's got eyes in the back of her head."

I shivered. It was only an expression, but we both knew anything could happen here at Emerpathy Middle, and the times it didn't were more not than often. But we couldn't sit there whimpering, which was why I said, "Okay. How 'bout we stick them underneath the tabletop? Like gum?"

"And that'll work?"

"I have no idea," I said. "But at this point, anything is worth a try."

I took one last look at Hamshaw—she was over by the Coke machine, waggling her finger at a kid who'd turned a brilliant shade of green—and I reached out and grabbed the pepper on my tray.

* * *

What happened next is something I will not forget. Not if I live to be a zillion, which, after everything I've been through, I'm not ruling out.

Just as my fingers closed around the pepper, a little tiny voice said, "Ow! Jou hurteeng me!"

I looked at Marty. His eyes were almost falling out.

"Please, tell me that was you," I said, but Marty shook his head.

Then, slowly, and with all the terror from a hundred-thousand nightmares about showing up at recess in your underwear, we both turned to the pepper on my tray.

Through tiny, twisted pepper-lips, it said, "Don' steeck me to the table, keeds. Jou gonna squeesh my head."

"It's talking," Marty squeaked.

"Jou right, I talking, mang. But don't tell nobody, or I gonna get een trouble."

"Your pepper is talking," Marty said again, in case I hadn't got that far.

"I not a pepper," said the pepper. "I am a preesoner of war. But I juse the deesguise-o-matic, and eet makes me look like thees. So I hescape. And someseeng else? Jou school ees not a school. Eet ees a sheep."

"A sheep?" I said.

"A space-sheep," said the pepper.

"How's it doing that?" said Marty.

"I study, een the language lab. But I make the meestake, and I learn espaneesh first, by watching Al Pacino movies. Jou understands me good?"

We nodded.

"Then leesten: Jou school ees go to outer space. Today. Real soon. With jou eenside eet eef jou don't do someseeng fast."

"Cool," said me and Marty, harmonizing.

"Jou theenk ees cool? Jou want to be stuck een the feefths grade for ten-thousands jears? I deedn't theenk so. So jou got to get us out of here. But sneaky-like, because the beeg fat lady? She's an alien."

"Mrs. Hamshaw?"

This made sense. It all made sense. My entire horrifying grammar-school experience was coming into painful focus.

"Our school's a spaceship," I said. "Our teachers are all aliens. That's why Mrs. Vinnaccio smells like plastic. It's why Mr. Bayers can't say 'dipthong' without spitting. And it explains that weird strip of hair thing Mr. Drake combs across his head."

"No, no, those guys ees juman being," said the pepper. "They jus' getteeng old. But they mind-controlled, so jou got to get us out of here, hokay?"

I'd say I thought about it all of half a second, maybe. And I will tell you: I don't usually take advice from lunchroom vegetables, but greater forces were at work here. That much was obvious, even to a kid.

"Let's go," I said, but Marty looked at me as if I'd grown a second head, and it was learning fractions.

"You're going to listen to a pepper?"

"Beats eating it," I said, and Marty couldn't argue. But we were going to need some help. Two kids like us would never get past Mrs. Hamshaw on our own. Not even in a lunchtime as stretched out as the ones at Emerpathy Middle School.

What we needed was a girl. Now, normally, it's against my policy to get too close to those, but this was an emergency.

"Kenzie Wertmiller," I said to Marty.

"She's over by the windows, sitting by herself."

"That's good," I said. "You ready?"

"Yeah. But what about my pepper?"

"Ees just a pepper," said the pepper on my tray. "But I

wouldn't eat it, mang. That theeng look like it make jou seeck."

* * *

Kenzie Wertmiller was a short kid, with glasses that eclipsed her face. She had hair the color of mashed squash, and the only way anyone would ever call her cute was if there was money in it. And that includes her mom. I tried looking nervous when we sat beside her, in the hopes that Mrs. Hamshaw would think I had a case of puppy-love. But Kenzie saw right through it.

"Get out of here," she said.

"Just wait a second."

"No. You called me plane-crash-face in gym. I mean it. You get out of here or you'll be sorry. I'm a paisley belt."

Marty made a face. "A what?"

"A paisley belt. It's like a black belt? Only better."

"There's no such thing," said Marty.

"You'll find out, fat mouth."

For such a little kid, she sure could argue. But we didn't have time for this. I noticed she hadn't touched her pepper, so I said, "You going to want that?"

She looked doubtful. "I guess I should. There's people starving in Cambodia."

Well, I'd heard that line a hundred times, at least, and I didn't buy it. I mean, there were people with headaches in New Jersey. Was I supposed to take an aspirin? Luckily for all of us, my pepper chose that moment to speak up.

"Thees ain't no time to play aroun'," it said. "Scary, scary theengs ees goeeng on."

I thought she'd scream. She didn't, though. Girls can be all right—sometimes. For instance, she just sat there with her eyes getting wider while the pepper told her why we had to leave the school, and she didn't say a word when I explained my plan.

* * *

Now, Mrs. Hamshaw would never let an ordinary kid go to the bathroom during lunch. But Kenzie Wertmiller was far from ordinary, and someday, she will win an Oscar. What I'm saying is, last time I saw anybody bawl like that was when I put a bunch of frog's eggs down my little brother's shorts. My parents grounded me. It worked on Hamshaw, too. The bawling, I mean, not the frog's eggs, although I would've tried them if I'd had a couple handy. Anyway, Hamshaw took Kenzie by the hand and led her out, and in minutes, we all met up again in the rotunda, near the front doors, with the pepper riding in my hands.

"I crawled out through the service hatch," said Kenzie. "Hamshaw thinks I'm in the bathroom."

The pepper squirmed. "Tha's good, keed. We go now, eh?"

We were on the verge of walking out, and I was feeling pretty good about it, when Kenzie had an attack of conscience.

"What about the other kids?" she said. "Like Brendan Scully. Timmy Howe. Joe Donnelly."

Marty raised his hand. "For the record? I never really liked Joe Donnelly," he said.

Kenzie's jaw, at that point, reminded me about a book I used to have on steamshovels. "Are you telling me that, knowing everything you know, you're just going to leave them here?"

She had a point. I'm not saying it stacked up against an eternity in fifth grade, but it was something.

"Oh, sure, the other keeds," the pepper said. "We gonna call the cops. They gets rescued. Hokay? Come on. Vamos!"

But Kenzie didn't budge. "The cops? What are we gonna say? Our lunch told us the school's in danger?"

She had another point. This one was bigger, and the pepper couldn't argue with it.

"I don't know," it said. "We talk about eet outside, hokay?"

"Come on," said Marty. "Let's get out of here."

I know, I know. I should have gone. I almost did, too, but the thing was, although I didn't like all the kids at school, like for example, Jimmy Cress, who poured Za-Rex in my roller skates, or Trisha Foss, who stuck her tongue inside my mouth that time, I didn't want them kidnapped into outer space, either. With a few notable exceptions. What if it was me? How would my parents feel? I mean after the initial joy wore off? I shook my head.

"I can't," I said. "I'm sorry. You go, Marty. Take the pepper with you."

I was surprised, almost, when Marty said, "Oh, great. Like I'm supposed to go alone? No way. I'll get captured in the parking lot, or something. I know it."

So we were staying. All of us. Not bright, maybe, but it felt right. Until the pepper started freaking out, that is.

* * *

"Jou keeding, right? I mean, jou keedeeng."

"We're gonna save the school," I said.

The pepper laughed. "Jeah? How jou ees gonna get past General K'Chazzpak?"

"General Ka-who?" said Marty.

"Chazzpak. He try to take over the juniverse, but he crash the sheep here twenty jears ago."

"The sheep?" said Kenzie.

"He means, 'ship,'" I said.

"He's a genius," said the pepper. "He juse the mind-control to make the people here forgets the crash. He makes the sheep look like a school."

Kenzie squinted. "It really sounds like he said, 'sheep.'"

"When the sheep crash, the computer break. Ever seence, jou keeds ees do the calculations. For to feex eet."

Marty looked like the guy on the Heimlich-Maneuver posters in the lunch room. "I knew my homework was too hard," he said.

"Hard? How many keeds jou theenk ees doing quantuum tenth-deemension reconciliations? Ees the cheesy walnut peppers. They got the mind-enhanceeng drug what make jou ten time smarter than jou was. And another theeng. They stretch the time out, so they get more out of jou."

This explained a lot.

"So we'll stop studying," I said, but the pepper didn't like it.

"There ees only one more computation for to be doeeng. They get that een a surpriseengs test they gonna geeve jou after lunch, and then the sheep take off."

"We'll flunk," I said. "On purpose."

"Jou theenk the other keeds ees gonna flunk? I telleeng you, we stuck here. We gonna go to war. And we ees gonna die."

The pepper started sobbing. It was pathetic, really, sitting there in the rotunda, listening to the blubberings of a depressive vegetable. I would almost rather do anything else at all, except possibly for certain tasks involving yard work or a toilet brush.

Thank God for Kenzie. She came up with the idea.

"What if we could change the tests?" she said. "Then the answers would be wrong."

The pepper's breathing hitched. "Jou know where they ees?"

She nodded. "One time, after school, I heard Mrs. Finnellini say they kept them in the library."

\* \* \*

We were walking down the hallway to the library, and I was feeling pretty hopeful about our chances for success when a familiar voice spoke up behind us, changing that.

"I changed my mind about the lunch money, punk," it said. "I'd like it. Now."

We turned around, and there stood Jinx. His real name was Henry Robb, but he'd punch you if you ever called him that. For that matter, he'd punch you if you called him Jinx, or if it rained, or if it didn't rain, or Mars went into retrograde.

At twelve years old, he had full facial hair, and although he wasn't what you'd call a smart guy, unless your arm was being twisted (which usually it was if you were standing close enough to him) he made up for his lack of brainpower by beating people bloody. He came walking toward me now, cracking his knuckles in a way that made me think of ice packs and methiolate.

"Who ees thees guy?" the pepper said, "and what happen to hees neck?"

Now, if we'd had brains, we would have run off screaming, but as for me, I thought Jinx would crumble at the prospect of a talking lunch, and I think the others thought so, too. What we'd forgotten was, Jinx was not like other kids.

"Hey, cool!" he said, and he snatched the pepper from my hands.

"You give that back," I said.

"Jeah, give me back!" the pepper said, but Jinx pushed me away. Telling him to do something was like beating up a pit-bull with a chicken.

"Hang on a second. This thing's awesome!"

"Give it back," said Kenzie. "I'm a paisley belt."

"Yeah, Good. Watch this," said Jinx. "You kids are gonna learn something."

I didn't doubt him that, whatever he was planning, we would find it educational, but I had a feeling we weren't going to like it. I was right, too. He reached into his back pocket, and pulled out a firecracker. He shoved it in the pepper's mouth, and then held up a lighter.

"This is going to be cool," he said.

And that was the first time I saw a paisley belt in action.

Kenzie may be small, but she's got feet of lightning. She kicked one of them up between Jinx's knees, connecting in a way that Jackie Chan would have admired. Jinx collapsed like my Dad that time I swapped his Hershey bar for Ex-Lax, and me and Marty turned to look at Kenzie.

"I told you, you'd find out," she said.

* * *

We explained everything while Jinx recovered. He insisted he come with us, "for protection," but for myself I wasn't sure if that was ours, or his. You wouldn't think he'd want anything to do with Kenzie after an attack like that, but he had hardly finished his recovery when he started offering to bring her books home after school. Anyway, we voted that we couldn't leave him wandering the halls with aliens around, and so he came along.

* * *

The Library at Emerpathy Middle School has never been my favorite place, just like my mom has never been a Pakistani carnival employee. For one thing, it smells in there. Like the dust of all the books on government and agriculture ever printed. And for another, the time goes even slower once you step inside. It's like being in church, or at my aunt's house, only magnified.

"It's quiet," Marty whispered. "Too quiet." Then he added,

"No, on second thought, it's just quiet enough. If it was any noisier, I wouldn't like it."

"Going somewhere, children?"

I almost screamed, for the second time that day. I turned, and there he was. 'Bad Hair' Day. The scourge of any kid who ever owned a library card. He was eight feet tall, and pear-shaped, with the worst haircut in history. He was quick with a 'shh' and he could spot a gum-chewer at 500 yards in the pitch black through a brick wall. Most of all, he hated letting kids inside his library. I think he was afraid they'd read something.

"Mr. Day," I said. "We were-"

"Doing research," said Kenzie, stepping forward. "We're doing a report."

Day smiled. "Oh, really? For whose class?"

"Mr. Fuller's," Kenzie said. "It's on ... dolphins."

"That's wonderful," said Day. "However, we don't allow food

in here." He nodded toward my pepper. "And secondly, the library is closed for lunch. You'll have to come back during a free period, or after school. Tomorrow would be best. As for now, I'm sure Mrs. Hamshaw must be worried..."

A free period? We were sunk. We'd never make it. And we couldn't let him take us back to Hamshaw.

That's when Jinx said, "You leave this to me."

Now, everybody knew that Mr. Day liked golf. He always talked about how great he was, and he kept a trophy on his desk. It had a little silver statue of a golfer on the top. He told everyone he'd won it in a tournament in college, though we were pretty sure he got it in a yard sale, and had his name put on it later. I only mention it now because this was the same trophy Jinx ran to and grabbed. "Hey, 'Bad Hair!'" he shouted. "You want this?"

You'd think the world was ending, or at least that part of it that held the library.

"GIVE THAT BACK!" Day tried to grab him, but Jinx dodged and made it to the hallway. He turned back, hooted once, and ran.

"You kids stay here," Day growled at us, and with that, he lumbered off in boiling-mad pursuit.

Marty, meanwhile, shrugged at me and Kenzie and the pepper.

"You heard the man," he said. "We stay."

\* \* \*

It didn't take us long to find the tests. The pepper thought if we changed one question on each one, the school would not be able to take off. That took a while, but time was something there was not a shortage of at Emerpathy, especially not during lunch. We changed the tests, put them away, and left the library. It went like clockwork. Marty even started whistling. He stopped, though, when Mrs. Hamshaw came around the corner, with Mr. Day behind her, dragging Jinx along by his right ear.

\* \* \*

Now, anyone who's never met Assistant Principal Gosling doesn't know their luck. The man is short and hunched and has a face that shows no evidence it wasn't hit repeatedly with a waffle iron. Emerpathy legend says, when he was born his first word was 'detention,' and it's been his favorite ever since. And on top of that, we'd soon find out he was an alien.

His office was a bare, cold place that sapped the hope from any kid who entered there. No cheery pictures brightened up the walls, no ornaments adorned the furniture. Unless, that is, you'd count the cheesy walnut pepper. It sat in a heavy plastic jar atop his desk.

"I sorry, keeds," it said. "We try."

In one corner of the room stood 'Bad Hair' Day, and in another, Mrs. Hamshaw smiled at us as fakely as she ever had. Next to her, Old Lady Plukrenge stared off into space, still carrying her ladle, her moustache twitching. Drool trickled from the corner of her mouth. And although her lips stayed shut, a voice came from the upper one. A voice that turned my guts to water.

"You children think you almost won, no doubt," it said. "Well you were never even close. Your friend, it seems, is not the only one with access to the disguise-o-matic."

"That moustache," Marty whimpered. "It's General K'Chazzpak!"

"Clever child," the moustache said. "And a few minutes ago, I was masquerading as a copy of The Guide to Modern Sweetcorn Cultivation in the library. Oh, I know you changed the tests. Don't worry. We can fix that. Now, Officer Gosling. Show them what they've won."

Gosling nodded. "Yes, General," he said. He reached up to his neck, as if to scratch it, but then he grabbed his hair instead, and lifted. Underneath, his bald skull gleamed.

"This thing," he said, waving a hand at the pepper, "may have escaped today, because we were so busy with our preparations, but we will never be so lax again. And you may rest assured that this ship will leave on schedule."

"After twenty years of waiting!" the moustache said triumphantly.

"The final data await processing," said Gosling. He pulled off one of his ears with a wet sucking sound and set it on his desk. "The other students ate their peppers. Even now they are digesting. Boosting their intelligence."

He removed his other ear, and then his nose, which he gave to Mr. Day.

"In sixth period, your classmates will take their 'tests,' and after that, the school will rise up from this stinking pit you call a planet."

He took off his lips. His cheeks. He put these in the 'in' box on his desk, and then popped out his eyes. They jiggled.

"You're coming with us," he said, his bare teeth shining in his naked skull. "And you're going to behave yourselves, and do your computations. And when we are out there, locked in interstellar war, no disguises will be necessary. And this is what you will obey."

He took his teeth and tongue out, and he set them on his desk. A thing slithered from the hole where they had been. It was fat and green and sluglike, and it slid up on his bony scalp and wobbled, looking down at us with eyes on stalks. It screeched.

Marty snuffled. Kenzie's breath went in and out in little wheezes. Jinx sobbed openly, and something small and warm and wet ran down my cheek.

And that is when Marty Ruckerman surprised us all.

"You can't take all of us," he said.

On average, Marty didn't talk like that, especially to adults. It shocked me even more when he jumped forward, grabbed the jar that held the pepper, and hurled it at the window. And believe me when I tell you, I had never seen a throw like that. Not in all my years of gym class.

Mrs. Hamshaw acted fast. She slapped a button on the desk, and a black shield slid across the window. But too late. The jar had smashed through. It fell outside, into the bushes.

"AFTER HIM!" the moustache shouted. "HE MUST NOT GET AWAY!!!"

A mad scramble for the door came next. Gosling put himself together hastily, and Day kept us four kids at bay while the faculty and staff ran out. "You'll pay for that, Ruckerman," he growled.

He slammed the door. We heard it lock, and we were left alone there in the office.

\* \* \*

I won't say I had a lot of hope. They weren't guarding us, but realistically, what could four kids do, locked inside an office? And what was one cheesy walnut pepper against a bunch of aliens and mind-controlled adults, even if it was bilingual?

"This isn't as bad as it seems," I said, although to tell the truth, I thought it might be worse. "My mom says it's always darkest just before the dawn."

"Your mom's never been awake at midnight," said Kenzie. "Just before dawn, it gets grey."

She was right, I knew. It wasn't until Jinx grinned at me that I realized we might still come out on top.

"The intercom," he said, with reverence.

I turned, and there, on Gosling's desktop, stood the chrome-pedestaled, white-buttoned microphone of the school-wide intercom. The one Gosling used for all his diabolical announcements.

"We can tell everyone," I said. "About Day! And Mrs.

Hamshaw, and the moustache, and the pepper!"

"Are you crazy?" Kenzie said. "You think they'll just believe us? Would you?"

I thought about that. She was right. Again. I was really getting sick of that.

"Well what else can we do?" I said. "We've got to tell them something."

Now it was Marty's turn to grin.

"Oh, we'll tell them something," he said, holding up the teeth and tongue that Gosling had forgotten. "But I don't think they're gonna like it."

\* \* \*

It took us a few minutes to get the hang of Gosling's mouth. You had to speak into one end of it, and anything you said came out the other end, in Gosling's voice. From there, we only had to aim it at the intercom. Jinx, meanwhile, shoved pennies in the door jamb to keep unwanted visitors away.

"This is Assistant Principal Gosling speaking," said Rucker-man, in Gosling's voice. "I want to assure you that we've fixed the problem with the cheesy walnut peppers. We only had a little trouble with the sewage pipes. Only a small amount of septic juice got in the oven."

"It was just a little bit," I added, taking my turn at

Gosling's mouth. "Nothing that could hurt you."

"And a teeny bit of barf," said Kenzie, "And a little beetle guts."

"And cigarette butts," said Marty. "And the washcloth Mrs. Finnellini uses on her legs."

We all looked at each other, and we nodded.

"But everything should be okay," I said. "If you think you're feeling sick, it's probably your imagination."

* * *

Emerpathy Middle School did not take off. Not then, anyway. It really couldn't, what with all the intelligence-booster drug being mopped up by the custodians later on that night. And everybody would have flunked their 'tests,' except they weren't around to take them. A bunch of kids ran off and told their parents about the food scare, and the board of health showed up, accompanied by six or seven news vans, and when we were discovered locked in the assistant principal's office with a couple human body parts, and when it turned out half the faculty and staff mysteriously disappeared, and the other half showed up delirious, the school was shut down pending state investigations.

The four of us went back there two days later—me, Marty, Jinx, and Kenzie Wertmiller—and we ducked the yellow tape.

We saw the pepper through the windows in the cafeteria, with about a hundred other gruesome looking lunches, sitting on a hundred orange plastic trays.

I knocked on the window. Two plates of chicken casserole and some dried-out pizza slices opened it.

"We going," said the pepper. "All of us preesoners of war ees takeeng off."

"Cool," said Marty. "Can we come?"

"No. Jou planet need jou. And anyway, we do the calculateeng now. Mos' of us ees smart enough. An' eet take us longer, but so what? We go a leetle slower. We got no war to fight."

"Well, it was great knowin' you," I said.

"Yeah," said Jinx. "Sorry about the firecracker."

"Will you leave soon?" said Kenzie.

"Tonight," the pepper said. "We make it look like ees a beeg hexplosion type of theeng."

"Cool," said Jinx.

"Maybe they buil' jou a real school. But jou watch out for Gosling and the General. Jou ain't hear the last of them, or of the beeg fat lady."

"Mrs. Hamshaw," I said. "She's got eyes in the back of her head."

"Mang, jou ain't keeding."

"But we've got us," said Kenzie.

"Right," said Jinx.

"And Kenzie's feet," said Marty.

"Ees good. I theenk jou be hokay. Just be careful what jou eat."

"Thanks for the advice," I told the pepper (and the other culinary refugees) "but from now on, I am planning on brown-bagging it."

*What is your life really all about? Will it ultimately be a tragedy or a triumph? You probably won't know until you're dead, and at that point, will you care? But even if it turns out to be a little on the MacBeth side, what then? Is the whole thing just not worth it at that point? The truth is more like what Jackson Browne says. "Nobody gets it like they want it to be." So true. But listen to that song. It's so joyous at the same time it tells us something sad. My favorite pieces of music are like that. They tell us the sad fact, but somewhere in the background, we can tell the musician is having a hell of a lot of fun. That's life, right there. That might just be the meaning of it, though it can never be put into words. Life is the happy melody behind the depressing lyrics.*

*This story has never sold anywhere, but I love it. It's hypnotic and fun, if a bit on the verbose side. It takes its time, so if you're not up for a long tale, skip it. But it ultimately goes somewhere dark and fun and funny all at once. Like life.*

# ELECTRIC FETTUCCINI
## SAMPLE CASE

The rain, owing to the altitude of the stormclouds, had fallen some twenty-thousand feet to land on the grass, tar, and gravel at the crossroads between route 28 and the Narrows Road in West Nazarad, Maine. The water molecules in some of the raindrops, before that, had been around the world billions of times since time began.

It seemed like sort of a wasted trip.

West Nazarad had never actually bored anyone to death. Not yet. In 1953 things had been touch and go for a while with a semi-retired mica miner named Nathaniel Groves. Nathaniel, who lived alone, had spent six months straight in a state of what seemed for certain at the time like pernicious lethargy. Around April, however, Claudia Briggs across the street had purchased a new set of curtains for her bathroom, which, unbeknownst to her, were rendered translucent, from Nathaniel's vantage point, by the peculiar angle of the setting sun against her window panes. Nathaniel therefore spent several tormented hours a week after that in conflict with himself over whether he should tell Claudia about the curtains or buy a set of new binoculars in Portland. Nathaniel never knew, therefore, how close he'd come to making a sort of twisted history, or how much he owed to the angle of incidence of certain solar rays and the curious oversights of a textile manufacturer down in Massachusetts.

Things had gotten duller in West Nazarad since then.

They were about to get a whole hell of a lot more exciting.

Some of the raindrops fell on a man in a broad-brimmed

black hat. He stood so still he would have made most statues seem in need of Ritalin. If there'd been a cereal called "Kellogg's Expectant Flakes," this man would've had his picture on the box.

He stood in the gravel of the soft shoulder, his eyes squinting at a spot of tar in the center of route 28.

He wasn't cold, nor was he wet, despite the rain, because of his coat, which had been woven from invisible, intangible strands of unadulterated desiccation, left over from some of the greatest droughts in history and collected through arcane methods at staggering expense from major deserts and then woven together by blind, necessarily insane, extremely danger-ous seamstresses in the black of night. It created around him a zone of dry so absolute it made his knuckles itch.

The particular spot of tar he stared at with such virginal an-ticipation contained a code that even now was translating itself. The code held information, in the polarities of the atoms in the chunk of tar and their electrons, protons, neutrons, and the fla-vors of their mutually annihilating and reforming quarks, that had lain dormant in those particles for a hundred-million years. The particles had come together, during that time, like the com-ponents of an organic, long-lived clockwork, meeting here at last from the sixteen-thousand corners of the universe on this night among all other nights in history. The chunk of tar was like a winning lottery ticket picked from all the other winning lottery tickets that had ever so much as dreamed of even hoping to exist.

The chunk of tar began to pulse.

The code within the matter that comprised the tar was self-translating, thanks to fifteen years of accumulated seismic power that now concentrated itself in the ground beneath this intersection. The intersection, by virtue of a patch, beneath it, of a strange variety of kinetically-absorbing schist, had been col-lecting minor tremors for the past decade and a half and stock-piling them, only to release them now in one controlled burst of energy, focused, through a sub-stratic parabolic area of granite, on that single spot of tar. The shock was recorded as far away as Eastern European Georgia, and was dismissed, initially, by the geologists who noticed it as a glitch in their equipment.

The man with the broad-brimmed hat barely felt the seismic power, by virtue of his shoes, which could absorb a blow the equivalent of the eruption of Vesuvius, if need be. The shoes, like the coat, had been made by processes and with materials normally hidden from the prying eyes and minds of modern man. They were, to say the least, almost painfully comfortable. A lesser man than their owner, upon wearing them, would probably have either wept to death from sheer gratitude or literally died of joy.

The chunk of tar began to glow in fits and flashes, like something about to cause a lot of trouble for the power company.

Using the law of conservation of matter and energy in a way that would have annoyed Einstein, fields of force appeared, created by a furious interaction between gravity, electricity, the weak and strong nuclear forces, and a misunderstood power that can only be described, unfortunately, as "gumption." The fields of force in turn created bands and interlocking, pulsing arcs of plasma, that shifted shapes and colors in such a way that they formed, briefly, a holographic representation of a sixteen-second, visual-only segment of a 1987 episode of Magnum, P.I. – to be specific, the episode where T.C.'s old war buddy dies of what turns out later to be a fabricated heroin overdose.

The brief excerpt from the eighties' detective show was just a side-effect, the real purpose of the light show being to create, by the synthesis of new matter out of purposefully perverted energy, first a skein of bone that grew, plantlike, branching, into a human skeleton, then quickly, blood (and veins and arteries to hold it), muscle, sinew, joints, synovia and sinuses, myelin and mitochondria, capillaries, synapses, scillia and follicles, all systems of a body overlaying one another, intertwining, bridging the organic gaps and growing into an accountant, five-foot-eight, with greased black hair, bespectacled, wool-suited, carrying a leather briefcase, and wearing on his upper lip what was arguably the worst moustache ever attempted to be grown by any living human.

He looked down at himself, taking a quick inventory of arms and legs and Rolex watch, looked up at the considerably taller man in the broad-brimmed black hat, and said, "Well it's about fucking time." After a pause, he added, "My feet are on the wrong legs."

It was true. The left foot curved away from the right, the effect of the two five-hundred-dollar wingtips ruined by the unnatural angles they cut with respect to one another. Furthermore, unseen and not to be discovered for at least another hour, the accountant had an extra, useless eye set in the middle of his solar plexus.

The man in the black hat put on a face that would have stumped a group-therapy session of retired Atlantic City croupiers.

"There wasn't time," he said, "to work out every little detail."

Had the accountant been drinking milk, it might well have wound up in little puddles on the tar, arrayed in a roughly cone-shaped pattern, with the apex at his feet.

"Time?" he said. "You've had a hundred million years."

"I've been busy," said the taller man, in dangerous tones.

"Busy, my ass," said the accountant, his sub-dermal capillaries dilating by the thousands. "If I know you, you couldn't wait until the seventies, so you could sit around watching reruns of The Courtship of Eddie's Father. If I know you, you couldn't wait for Oxycontin to be invented so you could get addicted to it."

The taller man held up a finger as if prepared to point it at the accountant and (possibly) to shake it disapprovingly. He didn't do this, though. In truth, there was a small supply of Oxycontin in a small black film canister in one of the near-infinite number of inner pockets in his desiccated suit. Even now he felt the subtle pull of it, demanding that he fix himself, but fighting the desire was easy, now, this close to the fulfillment of his current destiny.

The big man was named Tony, Pope Boniface III, Jack the Ripper, Bodhisattva, Ephram Smith, the butcher, the baker, that fat guy who lives down on Elm Street with his mother at age 34 when you'd think he'd just get a job for God's sakes, the thing from another world, "Bill," Mohammed, Jesus Christ. A hundred-thousand other names. And that was just on Earth.

He'd had a lot of names, a lot of lives, a lot of eternities on other worlds before this one. And immortality, he'd found, was worse than unendurable, unless you occupied yourself, which he did through his love of battling addiction. Heroin, nicotine, caffeine, Benzedrine, gasoline, Demerol, Phenobarbital, uppers, downers, marijuana, peanut butter, gambling, leche nuts, co-caine, and video games. Alcohol in all its many forms, of course: sloe gin, fast gin, gin martinis, top shelf, well drinks, cosmo-politans and all the variegated drinks and drafts. Methadone, the opiates, nitrous oxide, daytime television, absinthe, house-hold cleaning products, fashion, sex, adrenaline, and chocolate. These were just to scratch the surface of the miles-deep list he'd been addicted to on Earth and all the worlds he'd spent his time on over the many-chambered lifetime of the universe. When he'd run out of things to get addicted to, he'd invented more. Nicotine had been his baby. He'd spent entire eons developing the tobacco plant, cross-breeding it up out of nothingness over painstaking millennia. Crack had been his, too. He'd been proud of that. And one time, on another world, he'd invented an addict-ive language, whose victims died babbling beautiful sentences to one another, sentences that were wise and sad and gorgeously constructed, full of truths about the universe, but ultimately ravenous, devouring time.

His addiction was addiction itself, and not just that, but fighting it. His habituation lay in shaking off habituation. It filled him with an ebbing, flowing, eon-spanning rush that helped him while away the endless ages.

He'd been clean now for two weeks, only taking the Oxycon-tin from his pocket to stare at it, savoring his fledgling triumph over it, relishing the day he knew he'd start injecting it again. He couldn't wait. He lived to wait.

But to suggest that he was lazy...

He made a mental note to slam his fist down furiously on a

desktop sometime in the foreseeable future, as soon as one became available. The accountant was enough to make Mahatma Gandhi want to slap someone. It was easy enough for him, of course, impregnated as he was with a comprehensive future history of each new planet and then put to sleep for several hundred thousand years. For him, a hundred civilizations came and went in the time it took to check his twenty-thousand-dollar watch. If time was really money, the accountant spent it like a government.

But to the tall man, "Ralph," Cruella, John Wayne Gayce, Donatello, Tsing-Mai, and Marc Antony, time went by one painful moment at a time. Did the accountant know what it was like to live ten-thousand years in a succession of nearly identical seaside huts made out of palm fronds, subsisting on shellfish, naked to the waist from both ends, nobody to talk to unless he made them up, going insane, returning to normality, and going insane again, over and over until you start to look forward to the change of pace? Did the accountant know what it was like to invent successive systems of mathematics, art, music, sculpture, literature, and macramé, to get bored with all of them and throw them out again, to seek the meaning of life and then remember that you already know a thousand of them, to gnash your teeth until you wear them to the nubs and then grow new ones, not once and not a hundred thousand times but until you lose count somewhere around half-a-million? Did the accountant know what it was like to wait nine-hundred thousand years for civilizations to arise and then to watch them die, to fall in love and lose that love and fall in love again and lose that love again a million times until, when country music is finally invented, you write half of all the songs within it under an array of fabricated names and listen to the other half with an attitude approaching mild disdain?

The accountant did not know.

But to Mrs. Raveson-Hunt, Tchaikovsky, Lao Tzu, Dickens, Achmaad Ralaman, these things were part of life. Somebody had to mind the store. Someone had to stay awake, stay conscious, shepherd the various bits of far-flung information that, one day, would reform into the accountant. A molecule of carbon here, a stray quark there, all vital, all in need of care. The tall man had spent the entire span of ancient Egyptian civilization, for example, posing as a temple sweeper, while surreptitiously maintaining and guiding one crucial calcium carbonate molecule in an otherwise unimportant chunk of unfinished, imported Somalian granite. He'd spent a thousand years in prehistoric India, ministering to the petrified jawbone of a variety of prehistoric swamp donkey which contained within its ossified mandibular curvature a single but indispensable trace atom of selenium. And as for the unfortunate alignment of the accountant's feet, well, the tall man would have had to live out the entire nineteenth and twentieth centuries on the bottom of the Bering Sea to amend that undesirable situation, and in his opinion there was only just so far you could be asked to go.

And anyway, he thought simmeringly, he would in that event have missed a lot of episodes of The Courtship of Eddie's Father. Maybe all of them. Not to mention, *And then Came Bronson.*

Ah, well. The accountant, after all, would find out soon enough. Then they would see who was the lazy one.

The rain gusted on a raw wind. A few droplets pancaked into the accountant's lenses, making tiny ticking sounds. Behind them, his eyelids snapped like change-purses.

"It can't be helped now," he said. "Let's just get on with it."

"Amen and Salame to that," the tall man said.

They turned, following each other's simultaneous and identical leads, and walked toward an apartment building—a converted farmhouse adjacent to one corner of the intersection. The single streetlight at the crossroads colored its ostensibly white siding the exact shade of urine saturated with an overdose of multivitamins. It stood two-stories high, slate roofed, three lightning rods along the ridge, warm, blue TV light stuttering through plain grids of windows set with antique, slowly melting panes of glass like fragments from a bygone acid trip.

They walked up the steps, the tall man's near-infinitely

shock-absorbing shoes making no sound whatsoever as they climbed the peeling risers, the accountant's inverted wingtips clocking awkwardly off boxy planks.

"I'll knock," the tall man said.

He did.

At that precise moment, beyond the steel door he rapped against, beyond its grimed window and its dingy off-off-yellow curtain, in a fluorescent-lit kitchen whose formica cabinets listed westward as if yearning for the forests of their pre-processed youth, stood Brian Chen, sniffing the suspicious contents of a past-due quart of milk, 1960's era monster-movie underlighting on his vaguely oriental features from the open door of the refrigerator.

Brian hadn't felt the seismic shock of the accountant's manifestation in the street outside. Nor had anyone else within a hundred miles, despite the rattlings of dishes in the cupboards of some forty-thousand homes, the destruction of numerous picture frames as they were knocked off walls, leaks in plumbing sprung in basements, shattered windows, displaced shingles, and the sudden strange behaviors of a multitude of household pets.

The epidemic of ignorance concerning the existence of the un-natural phenomenon was the result of a seeming catastrophe of traumatic social coincidence. At the exact microsecond of the tremor, every conscious man, woman, or child within a hundred miles of the tremor's point of origin got an unexpected phone call telling them a close friend or relative had died, or else they experienced what felt like a massive heart attack, or else remembered they were missing an appointment crucial to the success of their career, or spilled the contents of their junior chemistry set all over their father's prized Laotian leather couch, or in some other way received the greatest shock of their life to date, only to learn a few seconds later that it had all been a mistake.

The phone calls were seemingly strange coincidences or pranks, the heart attacks were painful but otherwise harmless and anomalous poolings of synovial fluid in the sheaths around the lungs, the missed appointments were mis-remembered from other days, the chemical spills turned out to be composed of disappearing ink, but each of these experiences served to distract their victim while the tremor passed, and each ostensible coincidence was brought about by strings of converging and snowballing events, tracing their origins back to insignificant occurrences as tiny as the redirection of the path of a sole bacterium, as far back as the dawn of earliest prehistory.

All of this, of course, had cost the tall man a lot of time and effort, to greatly understate the situation. Business executives around the world would have loved to have his organizational skills, or, failing that, just a glimpse at the arcane and wondrous workings of his appointment book. There were entries in it like this:

Wednesday, November 14th, 2,415,723 BC, 3:14:34:48:03pm, cause a paremicium in Naples, France to change its course across the surface of a puddle three degrees, so as to create, through the ensuing chain of mounting circumstance, the apparent but illusory death in the far future of a woman named Katherine Alice Bryce.

You didn't have to be addicted to every addictive substance, lifestyle, or language known to every form of intelligent life that has ever occupied the cosmos in order to keep up with an infinite number of appointments like that. But it helped.

Brian Chen, meanwhile, put the open cardboard carton on the off-off-grey formica countertop near his Hotpoint fridge, and frowned.

"Jesus, how many cats can there be?" he said.

He said this because the last three times someone had knocked on his door after 8pm on a weeknight, they had previously hit and killed a cat out in the intersection, and had then decided Brian's apartment door looked like the most plausible place to start apologizing. He frowned some more, steeling himself against the expected barrage of fretful entreaties for forgiveness, navigated the potentially hazardous convolutions of his interior décor, stepped around his boots, grabbed the doorknob, turned, and opened.

The words "holy" and "mackerel" occurred to him, in quick succession. On the right, the tall man stood, completely dry, infusing Brian instantly with a potent but indefinable strain of déjà vu because, out of convenience, he had purposefully grown the wrinkles on his face into an exact and current (but inverted and only subconsciously recognizable) road map of Laconia, New Hampshire, a town he'd driven across the night before in a rented Hyundai, pulling over at each junction to consult his facial crenellations in the rear-view mirror. On the left, the accountant dripped, his eyes intense, clutching the handle of his battered leather briefcase as though it contained his folded soul.

The tall man smiled, his current mouthful of Mah-Jong-tile teeth stained an aging parchment hue by centuries spent smoking singular tobaccos. "Hi, there," he said, his voice like something grainy in a Cuisinart.

"You mind if we come in?"

"Who are you guys?" said Brian, who did mind.

"Insurance salesmen," said the tall man. "Census takers. Two guys who got a flat a few miles down the road. A pair of homicidal maniacs. Canvassers in the neighborhood collecting support to fight cutbacks in basic services like law enforcement, education, and local aid. Two incredibly remedial high school students on a nighttime bottle drive. A couple of believers, desperate to convert you to the church of Santeria. You wouldn't happen to have a chicken, would you? Of course, it doesn't matter what we say."

It didn't, Brian found. In fact, at that moment the tall man started talking about the increasing trend toward mass-market consumerism in North America and how the great washed, disinfected, exfoliated, and moisturized masses perceived it as normality. Brian tried to turn and run from this obvious demonstration of insanity, thinking of the kitchen phone and 911, but no sooner had his right foot begun to leave the mud-room floorboards than the tall man's industrial-hydraulic-clamplike fingers had him by the throat and through two belt-loops in his Carhartts.

"Jesus Christ," said Brian.

"Among other things," the tall man agreed. He lifted Brian off the floor as easily as if he were composed of hollow chocolate, a party favor for some strange and nonexistent holiday. He carried Brian like an effigy into the living room, then let go, but instead of falling, Brian stayed where he'd been put, his feet dangling some eight inches off the carpet.

The tall man stepped back, smiled. The accountant, who had followed, directed one equally weighted look each at the cream colored couch and the white pine coffee table, sat on the former, laid his briefcase on the latter. He clicked the catches, popped the top.

"Are you guys from outer space?" Brian somehow managed to ask.

The tall man made a noise you might hear on an advertisement for an antihistamine.

"Outer space," he parroted, disgusted. "These provincials. I've been here a hundred-million years, and still they don't consider me a native."

"Quiet," the accountant said. "I'm thinking." His hands were in the briefcase, or had been. They weren't strictly hands any more. They'd split apart at the finger joints, bifurcated, trifurcated, docadecaterafurcated into almost infinitely smaller branchings, lines of cool and dangerous light of deep colors from an eldritch wavelength, each as thin as a fraction of a fraction of a single strand of spider silk, each as curling and self-referential as an Arabesque sculpted over excruciating decades by a schizophrenic spatial genius. Just looking at the endless fractal puzzle in the briefcase nearly disintegrated Brian's head from the sheer confusion of the light and depth and intertwining color. It was some kind of a machine, in there, but Brian couldn't tell where it began and the accountant ended.

Brian lost all faith in any rational conclusion to the situation. In other words, he panicked. He didn't have to, and his panic didn't last.

The first reason for this was that he'd believed with growing consistency and certainty over the years that everything would work out for the best in the end. This erroneous conclusion was based on a fallacy: namely, that everything had worked out okay up to this point and therefore everything would continue to go well in the future. He saw his life, therefore, as a series of high and low-points stretching out to within spitting distance of infinity. He couldn't tell yet whether that series would have a value, in the end, that added up to positive or negative, in other words, whether his life would ultimately rate as a success or as a failure. But again, based on what he'd seen and done so far, he couldn't really believe that he was about to die.

The second reason Brian didn't think that he would die was faith. Put simply, like Martin Luther King, Brian had a dream. Unlike Dr. King's dream, however, Brian's was not concerned with social justice, but centered around a girl named Stacy Cooper, with whom he'd had what she described to people as "a thing" going for the past eleven months. In Brian's dream, he proposed to her in six more days, from one knee on the floor of Merzey Textile, Inc., where Stacy had a job as an assistant plant engineer. Also in his dream, they raised two children and moved to Montana (not necessarily in that order) where Brian opened up a freelance photography business. They both had decent careers in this dream. They didn't get rich, but neither did they go completely broke, and they lived comfortably, hiking, snow-boarding, traveling occasionally, retiring late, and then, in some distant, other life, they passed on in old age, with no regrets, their deaths caused by something peaceful, short-lived, and rela-tively painless.

The third reason Brian's panic didn't last was that his own fingers, at that moment, bifurcated, trifurcated, docade-caterafurcated, as did his toes within his athletic socks and the split-ends of his hair, into Supra-Gordian infinities of spider-web-thin light that pulsed with intermittent brightness, cas-caded to the coffee colored carpet, ran across it, twined organically up table legs, across the tabletop, and etched themselves up the outside of the accountant's briefcase, connecting at a hundred-thousand sizzling points to the complexity within.

This alone would not have calmed Brian Chen's fears, of course (the opposite was true) except that along the multiplicity of fibers came the electrical equivalents of subtle calming compounds, which served to mellow Brian's mood just enough to keep him conscious of his situation. Next came information, and with that information, Brian understood.

"It's better if you do this by a conscious choice," the tall man explained as understanding of the situation took Brian like a case of flesh-eating bacteria.

"I said be quiet," the accountant said again. "This is not as easy as it looks."

The tall man dropped his eyelids three-quarters of the way. "Fine," he said. "I'm going to make coffee. Want some?"

When the accountant didn't answer, but at length began to sweat and wince as though playing an impossibly difficult video game for the fate of every living creature in the universe, the tall man gave out a sound you might hear on an advertisement for a bronchial asthma remedy and turned and headed for the kitchen.

Brian's understanding, meanwhile, grew.

What Brian understood was this:

Things were not going to turn out all right.

That is, he was in no immediate danger from the two men he now knew as the accountant and the tall man. They would take nothing from him without his permission, and in fact they had expended almost unimaginable effort, traveling across mind-hammering gulfs of time and space, to offer him a deal the nature of which no other human being across all eternity would have the opportunity to take advantage of.

What he was in danger from was life itself.

From the briefcase, through the sprouting wilderness of uncountable electric pseudo-neuro-capillaries, Brian saw his future. He saw it with a certainty born of temporarily augmented mental faculties and instantaneously apprehended systems of abstracting thought as far above algebra and calculus as they themselves are above counting up to three on fingers. He saw that things would not turn out all right, not once, not twice, but over and over again in an ever-worsening pattern that would take his life ever downward into death.

For example:

Brian experienced, with a clarity of sensory input more bright and hard-edged than his normal waking life, an hallucination that depicted the very real and imminent disintegration of his relationship with Stacy. In just fourteen seconds, he lived through a pre-production of the next six months, over the course of which he and Stacy would discover previously hidden but irreconcilable differences between them. They would say goodbye, still friends, but crying in the café down the road, over their respective cupfuls of exotic teas, across a bentwood table from one another that, though only four feet in circumference, might as well have spanned a million miles from edge to mayonnaise-smeared edge.

After that, Brian knew with every pulsing cell of every harmonizing tissue in his body, he would live through eight interminable years of loneliness, dating sporadically but unable to find another soul with whom he felt he could connect. He would lose his looks during that time to a case of psoriasis so acute that afterwards he would seriously consider making extra pocket money as a sideshow freak.

Next, Brian saw with unquestionable fidelity and faith and growing madness, he would realize, at the depth of his loneliness, that it had only been the fear for his own well-being that had kept he and Stacy from their true destiny of marriage, kids, and cute old age together. In view of this, he would spend years studying strange but towering philosophies including but in no way limited to Greek Stoicism, Buddhism, Hinduism, Judaism, Catholicism, Tibetan Mysticism, and the spined but surprisingly acute wisdom of dockworkers in certain sections of Northeastern New Jersey. Finally, having mastered his own death, he would at last judge himself ready to love another, and, fearless, he would meet a woman named Lucille—a brilliant, loving, selfless (if not exactly attractive) turkey farmer from Western Massachusetts, with whom at last he might have found true happiness had not she died a year later from internal bleeding after being run down by a gas truck.

Brian, of course, would rail against the fates, the gods, luck, hope, charity, and Santa Claus—anyone and anything, in other words, who might have intervened but hadn't. And in the absolute zero of his soul, in the worse than senseless aftermath of her death, Brian would realize that, though he had conquered his death, he was not prepared to deal with the deaths of people close to him.

From such beginnings new worlds grow. Brian would leave behind his dreams of a photography business and, a decade late but filled with purpose, he would enroll in medical school, would spend long years in training, would know at last the triumph of a medical degree, an internship, a job at a prestigious hospital, years spent saving lives. But for each new life he saved, ten thousand more would die each quarter of a day on planet Earth, enough to fill four football stadiums a week.

And so the drinking would start, and Brian's fire would dwindle along with his success, until one day, face down in the stale sawdust on the pock-marked floorboards of a Boston bar, he would remember conquering his own death, and he would realize that he didn't literally have to save the lives of all those dying faceless billions. The thought would hit him like a 747, down there amid the peanut shells and never-to-be tasted, wasted, drying beer, that if he could help those billions to see that their own deaths were nothing to be feared, then they'd be free. Then Brian wouldn't have to worry about them any more.

And so again Brian would study, but this time he would study with a view to teaching what he'd learned, and he would write a book so short and sweet and simple, so easy to understand and yet so deeply wise and mind-releasing that it would unshackle every soul who read it from the fear of death, would cease all conflicts, and would unite the warring, violent nations under the colorless, ageless, sexless banner of love, had they all read it, which they never would because on the same day it was released a world war would begin.

Biological and chemical warfare on a global scale would decimate the population of the Earth, and Brian, bitter, old, decrepit, would die painfully of untreated cancer of the everything, disillusioned, in one corner of an unfurnished, cockroach-trammeled room in a condemned tenement house in Auburn, Maine.

Brian lived all this in forty-seven minutes, his eyes staring on in wordless horror, tears chasing one another down the smooth valleys in between his nose and cheeks, drool running on ahead of them and bungee jumping off his chin. He knew this vision of his future life was true beyond the cool spot in the shadow of a doubt. He knew this was his future life because the functions of his brain had been expanded, such that he could see and touch and taste and feel the branching streams of future time as incontrovertible equations, all solved and proven, without the merest possibility of error.

"Doesn't look like fun," said the accountant, "does it?"

Brian made a small, weak sound.

"The thing is," the accountant said, "you have a choice."

Brian made another small, weak sound. This one was more plaintive than the first had been, and included consonants.

"I can change it?" Brian said.

"Well, no," said the accountant. "But don't let that discourage you. What I mean is, everything is unavoidable, and fated, yet at the same time you have a choice. Freewill. It's a paradox, I know, but so is life. And we could make you understand the paradox, but that would mean increasing your mental capabilities to such a degree that it would probably prove fatal."

"You mean," said Brian, "You could tell me, but you'd have to kill me."

The accountant's eyebrows moved together, crinkling the flesh between them.

"Not exactly," he said, "but you get the general idea."

Then the accountant shut his eyes, and flicked a hundred million nonexistent switches, and a feeling hit Brian like all the concentrated happiness from a thousand childhood picnics, and then it went away again and the accountant said, "We can give you that. A diluted version, of course, but it would last until the day you die. You'd still experience all the pain and suffering, the deaths, the failures, but this would run underneath it all. Joy. 99 and ¾ percent pure. All you have to do is say the word."

For reasons Brian couldn't have immediately articulated, he felt the natural wariness of a man in the vicinity of a used car salesman.

"Let me think about it," he said.

* * *

It doesn't take an hour to make coffee, unless you are the tall man. He'd been re-brewing it with fresh grounds again and again and cooking it down, until he had a pot of something that resembled used motor oil in both color and viscosity—the caffeinated beverage equivalent of crack cocaine. The fumes convecting upwards off its tar-pit surface made his eyelids sting. Just a whiff of this questionable ingestible would be enough to keep a normal man unnaturally alert for several hours.

"That's the stuff," he said, gripping the pot's handle, and he poured some of its syrupy contents into one of Brian's mugs. The mug said, "Keith" on it for reasons too complicated to go into here, and the glaze on its interior started breaking down immediately into its component molecules.

The tall man took a sip.

The ostensible coffee coated his esophagus like enhanced Pepto-Bismol. The caffeine launched into his bloodstream like a flood of traffic through an inner-city interchange five minutes after work lets out. A normal human would quite possibly have had an aneurysm from the sharp-edged biological reaction, but the tall man, if asked, would have called the feeling, "mildly refreshing."

In the adrenaline-assisted sharpness of his currently accelerated state of mind, the tall man bent down over Brian's stovetop, which was smeared, on a microscopic level, with the invisible remains of fifteen years of bygone dinners. He focused specifically on the right, front burner, on a stainless-steel measuring cup that rested on the heating coils, on the yellow, phlegmy liquid in the cup, sizzling and gently frothing.

The tall man slid his free hand within the mazelike contortions of his desiccated overcoat. After a few moments of uncertainty, he withdrew a graduated hypodermic, which he used to siphon up the bubbling drug.

With a movement that had taken several centuries to master, perfected to the point that even the most observant of cynical magicians would have missed it, he slid the hypodermic up his sleeve.

He smiled. A Mah-Jong fanatic, had there been one there to see it, would have felt uneasy at the sight.

The accountant was about to go on one hell of a ride. The tall man, who saw himself, if only momentarily, as a sort of disturbing carnival employee tearing tickets on the entrance platform of the great Ferris wheel of life, was going to send him on it.

He'd been planning this for the past ten thousand years.

He took another sip of supra-coffee, poured a cup for the accountant, and stepped through the open doorway to the living room.

"Finished?" he said, smiling.

The accountant gave him a look. If he'd had eternities in which to study human nature and facial expressions like the tall man had, the look would have conveyed a feeling of near-contempt mitigated by his own abundant self-uncertainty. As it was, it just looked squinty.

"He's making up his mind," said the accountant.

"Well. In that case, coffee."

The tall man placed the cup atop the coffee table, where it sent up noxious airborne pseudopodia of toxic steam. The accountant eyed it with suspicion. The tall man, meanwhile, sketched a glance at Brian, who still hung on nothing in the center of the room and, at that moment, could have passed for a badly exposed, poorly focused, life-sized photograph of his former self.

"He's taking it well," the tall man said, by way of making conversation.

"Is he?" said the accountant, by way of quashing it. "I wouldn't know. I haven't been human for as long as you."

The tall man shrugged. The accountant had him there. Poor, lost soul that he was. The tall man almost regretted having to get rid of him.

The accountant, meanwhile, who was not in such a warm and fuzzy state, unbuttoned his still-damp suit jacket and the white shirt underneath it, to reveal the extra, useless eye that stared out of his solar plexus.

"Look at this," he said, with venom.

"Oops," the tall man said.

Anyone might reproduce the expression that next appeared on the accountant's face by slamming a hatchback door shut on the second knuckle of their pinkie finger.

"Oops?" he said, as if trying to be heard across a crowded room. "Oops? You put my feet on the wrong legs, you put an extra eye in my stomach, and all you can say is 'oops'?"

The tall man's bushy eyebrows lifted. "I told you, I was busy."

"Busy." The accountant made a porcine sound. "I do my job. I suppose it's too much to expect the same from you. I only get a few hours on every world we visit, you know. The least you could do is see that I'm put together correctly."

The tall man's fledgling pity dissipated instantly. "You know your trouble?" he said. "You're afraid to live."

Power-hammers don't hit nails on heads with such precision. The tall man saw how close to home his words had struck by the millimeters-increase in the whites of the accountant's eyes. But behind the eyes, behind even the portion of grey matter that currently housed the accountant's conscious mind, deep within the system of habits and ingrained memories and opinions and beliefs and electro-bio-chemical reactions that, in collusion, made him who and what he was, the accountant felt the psychic blow. Defense mechanisms flung themselves up inside his mind in rapid-fire succession: anger, scorn, amusement, even pity. But at a level deeper, even, than he visited in his most easily forgotten dreams, the accountant had been struck.

Across the spans of walled-off synapses, miniature lightnings fired—the barest harmonics of subconscious thought, wherein the accountant felt and knew himself. The data resonated, down there in that sub-Stygian mental abyss, that no single and traumatic happenstance had rendered the accountant terrified of life. Rather, an ordered chaos of both chance events and chosen courses had grown organically within him, each new factor building on the sum total of the ones before, making him (by exponentially increasing graduations) continually more afraid.

The accountant, of course, had had his memory destroyed on taking up his current job, but he knew that there were buried traumas, childhood horrors, poor choices, and unfortunate parental actions lurking in his past. The sum total of his life and of the millennia before he had existed had conspired, in him, to create a living, thinking being who, for a million microscopic reasons, saw life as a dangerous, unfriendly thing that had to be subdued, controlled, kept at arm's length, and if possible, caged, shot, hung, disinfected, buried, and then exorcised by a religious official from every belief system—major, minor, and otherwise —in existence. Life, in short, was dangerous.

It was the single biggest cause of death, after all, and death was a serious problem. The majority of all intelligent life forms were now dead. Just thank whoever was in charge the dead were not allowed to vote.

The accountant, cognizant of this, not consciously but to the deepest inner workings of his soul, had backed away from life at breakneck speeds. Somewhere in his now nonexistent memory had been a record of a span of life spent becoming increasingly mechanical. Regimentation had taken over the accountant's life.

He had surrendered to a self-micromanaged routine voluntarily —had become the most famous living numbers-cruncher in the known universe, had performed feats of processing previously unattempted, had tracked heretofore untraceable currencies through tracts of financial space so trackless and unchartable, created by such consciousness-blasting uber-corporations and systems of arcane and theoretical mathematics, that those few daring beings who had tried the feats before had ended up insane, their minds lost and wandering through abstracted monetary landscapes.

But the accountant had trained his mind, had honed it, shaped it, crafted it. His intellect had become a work of art, a place of convoluted clockworks that could twist and bend with such agility that no brunt or torrent of mere data could perplex it.

And then one day, a hundred universes earlier, he had lost it all.

It had been a tough assignment, to be sure. He'd been charged with creating an assessment of the financial status of a corporation that existed in nine different universes simultaneously. Just understanding all the self-negating systems of mathematics such a task entailed had necessitated that he grow six extra, supra-dimensional heads with which to learn them. Navigating all the streams of mutually annihilating data was the single most difficult feat of abstracted engineering ever attempted, according to those working closely with the project.

It had proved too much for him. The accountant had gone insane, had lost even his ability to figure simple equations in nineteen dimensions, had lost his entire clientele in the time it usually took him to digest his lunch.

In the dark time following the mental cataclysm, the accountant had recovered to a shadow of his former self, and he had thought long and hard about his life and what he wanted from it, and he had realized that unless he did something now to change, he would die the same regimented, living, thinking robot he had been for as far back as he could cast his mind.

What he needed was a break. Excitement. Adventure. Change of pace. He needed spontaneity. To see new sights. To live. Finally, to live.

"Maybe I am afraid to live," he said.

The tall man squinted, his inverted facial map of Laconia, New Hampshire crinkling in non-topographically accurate ways. "Maybe?" he said. The squint deepened. Had the map possessed the power to affect the territory, thousands would have died in sudden earthquakes. "Maybe you're afraid to live? What are you, Lord God of all understatement? Look at yourself in the mirror sometime. You don't live. I wake you up once every hundred million years or so, to do the same thing, over and over. You're like a cognizant TV commercial, with an extremely low budget."

The accountant's eyes tracked back and forth, following the action of an unpleasant little fast-paced movie in his mind. The tall man was correct, of course. And even this job, which was supposed to let him experience life and have adventures—which was supposed to bring him out of his shell and broaden him— had failed. He wasn't living. He had never lived. He was never going to live, unless...

It came to him with all the subtlety of a sales pitch for a health and beauty product in a television infomercial. He saw a way, suddenly, where he might truly live. Of course, the tall man would have to go, but he could arrange that without too much difficulty. Anyway, the tall man had always been a royal pain in his intra-species ass.

"Well," he said. "Let's get this finished, anyway."

The tall man ran his fingertips across the stubbled skin beneath his mouth. "I couldn't agree more," he said.

With that, they both turned back to Brian.

* * *

What the tall man had no way of knowing was that the accountant, eager to sever their relationship and the bonds of his current employment, had prepared a packet of neuro-coded (albeit temporary) super-strength that, when he released it into his nervous system in a short while, would render him capable of subduing the tall man. Beating him senseless and leaving him in a puddle of his own frustration, never to recover. This packet hung in the back of the accountant's mind, needing for him only to think the word, "rigatoni" before it would bloom and blossom, shoot through his neural conduits, transform his muscles, and turn him (again, momentarily) into a physio-psychic powerhouse.

He was only waiting for the right instant. And it was fast approaching.

* * *

Through the countless massless conduits of light that still connected him to the accountant's briefcase, Brian was bombarded, at that moment, with another sense of understanding. This time, what he understood, not only to the roots of his hair but to the deepest depths of every living cell within his body, was that the accountant and the tall man had traveled unimaginable distances across vast spans of time in order to allow him to experience a constant thrum of subtle joy, and all they wanted in return was to take away his misery. The choice was put before him plainly. All he had to do was to say, "Yes."

"No," he said.

The infinity of illuminated arabesques inside the briefcase flickered. The tall man cocked an eyebrow.

"Are you serious?" he said.

Brian was dead serious. "The way I see it, if you've come all that way to take away my misery, there must be something awfully special about it."

Like most people, Brian had absolutely no idea.

Brian had no idea that the accountant and the tall man weren't after his misery, per se, but after his capacity to experience misery. After all, he was, at this moment, probably a lot happier than he would be at certain later stages of his life.

Likewise, he had no idea that his capacity to feel misery, by most measurements, wasn't all that special. There were billions of people who had lived or were still living on planet Earth who were, or who had been, a thousand times more miserable than Brian could ever hope to be.

Further, Brian had not the slightest clue that his capacity for misery, in another way, was perfect because it and only it could cure a sort of terminal, degenerative disease that afflicted a higher being who existed several universes distant from Brian's, who would pay for it a price exorbitant to the point of being incomprehensible to most sentient beings.

To add to this, Brian didn't know all sorts of other things, like for instance that the tall man and the accountant had arrived on Earth a hundred million years ago, or that the tall man had tinkered lovingly with the previously existing ecosystem, encouraging the human race to grow and thrive, making a small change here, a tiny alteration there, until the human race brought forth the perfect specimen in Brian. Or, for instance, that the human race was only one among a hundred thousand species that the tall man had likewise instigated and encouraged on as many worlds, taking from each one a single, perfect capacity to experience emotion as a similar geriatric remedy to disease in distant, unimaginable, semi-deities. Or that the accountant's job was to collect and log Brian's capacity to feel misery, or that he would then go back to sleep for another several hundred thousand years, while the tall man went back to semi-aimless and addicted wandering. Or that, when the human race had evolved their civilization to the point where instantaneous and unlimited travel was at its disposal, the tall man and the accountant would leave Earth, would deliver the remedy to the higher being, and would move on to the next job. Or that the human race would, at that time, join the wider universe, the price for its creation paid in full.

There were an infinity of other things that Brian didn't know. His ignorance was like a god in its ubiquity. But among the few things Brian did know was that he recognized a sketchy sales pitch when he heard one, and that he wouldn't let his misery go now for all the money in the world.

"It's not for sale," he said.

The tall man kept his jaw from dropping by an act of superior self-mastery, the likes of which had not been seen on Earth since the days of Alexander, whom, incidentally, he had been. "What do you mean, not?"

"I mean I'm not selling," said Brian, gaining strength, gaining faith in himself, gaining fervor. "I mean come back some other time. I mean thanks for the sales call, but I'm not interested, ask somebody else."

The accountant, who knew about the singularly Earthling practice of telemarketing through his instantaneous, comprehensive pre-mission briefing, frowned and said, "There is nobody else."

"All the more reason for me not to sell," said Brian. "Manhattan sold for a pair of pants. The Louisiana territory went for peanuts."

"Both sums are historically inaccurate," the tall man said. He stripped out of his desiccated overcoat because, suddenly, he was feeling warm. He hadn't had a subject refuse to sell in universes of time. "But if you want more, there is a precedent."

"Screw your precedent," said Brian, feeling suddenly triumphant. "I don't even know what I have, so I'm sure as shit not selling it to you."

The accountant's terrible moustache twitched. "Come on Brian," he said. "Whatever doesn't kill you makes you stronger."

"Right," said Brian. "Unless it turns you into a paraplegic or a mental vegetable."

The tall man's lungs released a sigh of epic pointlessness. "Think about this, Brian," he said. "The rest of your life is going to be terrible. You saw it. You know it's true. Why not be happy?"

Brian, who had wondered about this sort of thing his whole life, now knew the answer to that question. "Because I don't have to deal with my whole life right now," he said. "Right now all I have to deal with is right now, and you guys. And I'd say if I can deal with you two and your electric fettuccine sample case and your extra eyes and anti-gravity and whatnot, I can deal with anything. And that's a pretty frigging powerful feeling, so let me reiterate: don't let the door hit you in the ass on the way out."

It was a triumphant moment for Brian. Never before had he felt so terrified, and yet never before had he felt so powerful. Finally called on the carpet and put in harm's way, he was finding out that he was constructed a lot more durably than he'd previously thought.

The tall man, meanwhile, didn't look impressed. "Well, I said it's better if you make the choice yourself," he said. "I didn't say it was the only way."

At that moment, the accountant walloped Brian with everything he had, which was quite a bit. Brian's muscles tensed in perfect unison, with such force that he threw himself into a fetal position, shook, and nearly knocked the coffee table over. The tall man took a step backward and frowned slightly, his hypodermic-finger twitching in anticipation.

"Did you have to hit him with so much?" he said.

"Be quiet," the accountant said. And through the million monofilaments came Brian's capacity to feel miserable, one electric dribble at a time, until all of it had been sucked away and stored in geo-holographic form.

"Well, there," said the accountant.

Brian, meanwhile, hung in the air, feeling like a giant ear that's just been cleaned. His mind, suddenly, was like a sitcom from the 1950's—all happiness, several centimeters deep but bright and shiny as all hell. And it felt good. No, things were not going to turn out well for him, but he found, suddenly, that he didn't care. He felt... he felt... swell.

"Thank you very much," the tall man said. He rammed the hypodermic into the accountant's neck and thumbed the plunger home.

Several things happened next.

* * *

The tall man felt instantly triumphant. For every moment of his long, long, unimaginably long adulthood, he had been addicted to everything remotely possible for him to be addicted to. And for all that time, he'd dreamed of kicking his main addiction, his major malfunction, the addiction to addiction itself.

He knew, however, that such a feat would require him to possess an emotion so pure and perfect it would shut out everything else, and here it was at last in Brain's fledgling misery. He could have waited, of course, for the accountant to go to sleep again, but by then their superiors would know the misery had been collected, and other complications would ensue. He felt sorry for the accountant, but there it was. When you're faced with the sum total of your wildest dreams within arm's reach, you take it.

He stepped back, watching the accountant shudder and waiting for the Oxycontin to take effect.

* * *

"Are you insane?" said the accountant.

He said this because, on the one hand, he had only recently decided to steal Brian's misery himself, to use it to experience what real life was really like. But he said it also because the drug was even now attacking him and rendering his brain unpredictable and ultimately useless. And as his mind turned into the cognitive equivalent of sushi, he lost control of Brian's misery, which he had yet to seal away inside his enigmatic briefcase. The resultant vacuum, meanwhile, pulled Brian's mind forward through the million conduits of light.

* * *

Brian felt himself yanked off center. He still looked out through his eyes, but he did it from a distance, now. The "him" that usually resided somewhere in between his ears had been stretched and strained as if through mental cheesecloth, and now largely occupied a spot halfway between his body and the coffee table. He could feel before him, as if through the haze of nonsense at the fringe of sleep, a set of paths that led to another mind, a someone else with whom he blended now by exponentially increasing increments.

The someone else was having trouble, and was clutching desperately to something Brian recognized as his own broken heart. And Brian knew in that moment that he could take it back. All he had to do was to reach out, and it was his.

He reached out.

A mental blow knocked him back. The accountant, down but not yet out, still had enough brainpower to deal with forty Brians. Brian suddenly felt pain as though his entire being were composed of fingernails and each one had a sewing needle hammered underneath it.

His universe spun in complicated anti-patterns. He reached out, trying to grab hold, and encountered something like an open passageway.

"Stay away from that!" the accountant snapped, crocodile-like.

Brian lunged. He gripped the somethings in the passageway, and pulled them out with every bit of strength he had.

They were copies the accountant had made of other emotions he'd collected. Thousands of them. Most of them were kinds of misery. Brian hurled them all in the direction of the accountant's mind, and tried, mentally, to duck. In among them, he found something he did not recognize as a neuro-augmentation packet, broke it open, and felt a wash of super-strength flood through his body.

The blast knocked the accountant backward through the sheetrock between two wall-studs, and out through the siding. Thin flaps of vinyl shivered around him, storklike, as he traced a lean parabola above the crossroads, landing out there somewhere in the rain.

The briefcase and its contents instantly went black. Brian fell to the floor like a sack of suddenly released potatoes in a pair of pants and a Van Halen T-shirt.

"Jesus Christ," the tall man said.

"I thought that was you," said Brian, who'd caught a glimpse of everything the accountant knew, and he stood up, grabbed the coffee table by one end, and swung it like Ikea's version of a God's-wrath baseball bat.

It hit the tall man and snapped violently in half.

"Out!" said Brian.

The tall man cowered, retreating toward the door. "You blew it!" he shouted. "You'll never be happy now, plebe!"

Brian snatched an end-table and brandished it.

"Git!"

The tall man ran into the door, rebounded, grabbed the handle, turned and pulled and ran out in the rain.

And how did Brian feel, at his successful rejection of a life of promised happiness in favor of an assured slide downward into total misery?

Like this:

One day, years ago, in Chinatown, New York, he'd bought and cooked a bitter melon and had found it to contain all the awful of a thousand grapefruits, like having the soft parts of your mouth simultaneously dehydrated in an industrial machine and sucked out through a tiny metal straw. Deciding he had made a misstep in its preparation, he had later asked his grandfather to explain the proper cooking method for the Oriental vegetable. The old man, perpetually smiling as if steeped in pots of boiling joy (though he had lost more close loved ones in his time than there are Tic-Tacs in a box) had gripped one of his grandmother's throw pillows by the outsized, macrameed buttons and spun it (which always sent her into fits of multilingual yelling) and said, "Supposed to be bitter."

When Brian asked him to explain, the old man, still smiling as if physically unable to prevent himself from doing so, said, "If not bitter, not good."

"But why eat it?" Brian asked, in the carelessly curious way of one who senses the tragedy of his own lost heritage but is unable to repair it.

"Because," his grandfather said, still spinning the pillow and if possible with his delight turned up a notch, "we eat from the yang."

Those two phrases came back now, from a grandfather long since entered ghosthood, with his yapping pomeranian of a wife and the pancreatic cancer that had taken him and all the endless loss that life invariably dishes, booby-prizelike, to those who live long enough, like an overzealous host still ladling the green beans almandine although you've got one hand on your belly and the other up, palm out and warding.

"If not bitter, not good."

"We eat from the yang."

And it occurred to Brian that the bitterness of misery could also be savored. That you could eat life from the yang. That every fraction of a moment, whether packed with joy or misery, could go down appreciated, like a gleaming challenge to whatever gods were looking on, from their immortal roadhouse bars in mild interest, bitter as a thousand bitter melons, blazing like a million grapefruit-centered sun. Yes. Send more. I like this.

Thanks.

He stood looking out through the fat raindrops turned urine-yellow by the streetlight's glow, and watched the tall man's figure dwindle, running.

*A man needs a pair of wingtips. Do you have one? And isn't it frustrating when you buy something on good faith and then it turns out to be defective? The good thing about that is, most companies these days will bend over backward to make you whole. Just don't push it.*

# HOW I GOT FREE SHOES

I once had a pair of shoes that squeaked so loud they annoyed beings in another dimension. I was informed of the problem by a lawyer the beings had retained. His name was Bartlett, and he manifested his presence on the steps of my trailer home one cold day in October.

"What dimension are they from?" I asked him, having been made aware, by the man, of the preliminaries.

"I'm afraid I'm not allowed to divulge that information," he said, snipping the end off a cigar. "But I can tell you they exist on a plane so far removed from our own that simply to contemplate them would drive a sane man mad."

"And are you mad?" I asked. I figured it was the obvious question.

"Most certainly not," he informed me.

"And why not?" I asked. "Haven't you been contemplating these beings?"

"Most certainly not," was his impassioned reply.

"Then how do you speak to them?" I asked him. "I mean, how did you find out they were annoyed by my shoes?"

"A fair question," he told me, "and one that has an equally fair answer. They called me on the telephone."

"What," I said, "from Dimension X?"

"I never said it was Dimension X."

"You never said which dimension it was at all."

"Exactly," he said. "And I omitted this information purposefully, because I am not at liberty, as their litigator, to divulge it, as I have already explained."

"Well," I said, "It's all a little vague, to me. I mean, it's perfectly fine for you to show up here on my steps and claim that some creatures from the tenth dimension—"

"I never said it was the tenth dimension."

"—are annoyed by the squeaking of my shoes, but—"

I paused. Looked around.

"Where was I?" I said.

"Right there," the man said, pointing at me.

Let this be a lesson to you. Never ask a rhetorical question within earshot of a lawyer.

"I can't understand why you're being so difficult," was what the man chose to say to me at this time. "I mean, after all, it's not as if these certain unnamed beings, from a certain, unnamed dimension, are suing you for damages."

"Well then, what are they doing?" I asked him.

"They're appealing to your sensibilities as a sentient, reasoning, enlightened intelligence. They wish you, simply put, to stop wearing the shoes."

"I don't understand," I said. "Are they really that loud?"

The lawyer finally got around to lighting the cigar, which he did with one of those new windproof lighters. After he had ensorcelled himself in a significant sphere of bluish carcinogen, he said, "Let me explain this to you."

"I think you'd better," I said.

"There is a wormhole," the man said, "stuck in the material of one of your shoes."

"Which one?" I asked him.

"I don't know that," he said.

"I've never seen it," I said.

"You wouldn't," he told me. "It's a very small wormhole."

"It'd have to be," I said. "How did it get there?"

"Poor workmanship."

"Really?"

"Would I lie about a thing like that?"

"I guess you'd be silly to."

We sat there and looked at each other while our respective trains of thought chugged along their respective tracks.

"So," I said, "What does this wormhole do?"

"It transmits sound," the man answered, "to the—to a certain dimension which shall remain nameless."

"And this sound is very annoying to certain interested parties," I closured.

"It drives them right up their extra-dimensional equivalent of a wall."

"Hm," I said.

"So you can see the problem," said the lawyer.

"I certainly can," I said. "But what's the solution? I mean, I can't just stop wearing the shoes. I'll admit they're not Armanis or anything, but they cost me sixty bucks down at the Rockport Outlet, and they're the only wingtips I've got. A man needs a pair of wingtips. Surely as a lawyer you can appreciate this."

"I can," he said, nodding in that way people nod when they can afford to concede your point because theirs is bigger. "But I can also appreciate that these certain unnamed beings could wipe out our entire galaxy as easy as blowing their nose."

"They're that powerful?" I said.

"Oh, yeah," he said. "Did you read in the newspaper last week about that star that went supernova?"

"They did that?" I said, impressed.

"No," he admitted. "But not because they couldn't have, if they'd wanted to.

I nodded.

"And there's no chance of me plugging up this wormhole," I said hopefully.

"The lawyer laughed.

"What," he said. "With some interdimensional bondo? I'm afraid we don't have the technology. No, the only solution is for me to take your shoes to a soundproof room deep in the earth, beneath a specially prepared mountain in Nevada, where they will sit until the end of time."

"That's going to make it hard for me to wear them to job interviews," I pointed out.

"These beings," the lawyer went on, "have, however, offered to make it all worth your while."

I became slightly more alert.

"Really," I said. "Like, how? Money? Fame? Power? You know, I've always wanted a time machine."

"They are going," he said, producing a contract from somewhere within his cheaply tailored suit, "to purchase for you, at their own expense, not one but two pairs of shoes, with their individual values not to exceed that of the present pair."

"What, is that all?" I said.

"That," said the lawyer, "and they'll promise not to turn the galaxy and all the planets and beings therein into a vast cloud of superheated gas."

I sniffed.

"You don't say," I said.

"I do, too," he told me, and he handed over the contract.

*I wrote this story about a day before I wrote the title story in this collection. It's got a nice little Zen feel to it. It encourages you to roll with the punches, no matter what happens. I sold it to an online magazine in the late 90s for a pittance, but I really like it. It'll show you what to do if you ever run into a...*

# TOURIST FROM THE
# TENTH DIMENSION

"To know is to not know," said the Interdimensional K'nagg Beast from the planet Paang, "to not know is to know. Did you know that? If so, how? Maybe you'd better sit down."

"I am sitting," I said, looking up from my bowl of oatmeal at its numerous eyes like black sapphires, bunched like grapes.

"Well, then, maybe you'd better stand up," it said. "It's hard to tell with creatures such as yourself, with your willy-nilly customs and your odd little language."

It took a picture of me then, or the Interdimensional K'nagg Beast from the planet Paang's equivalent of a picture, which was accomplished, in its manner, by holding up a small, photoelectric creature that looked something like a hamster, and biting off its head. It explained the process to me later, over beer and wheat-nuts at the local watering-hole, but as for now it just waved a feeler at me and said, "Please, go on with what you are doing. Pretend I am not even here."

I have to admit that its soft-spoken suggestion left me at somewhat of a loss for words. It is one thing for a roughly centipede-shaped creature to materialize into existence in the kitchen of your trailer-home and stand towering over your dinette-set, dripping a sort of syrupy ichor from its six-inch fangs. It is yet another for it to suggest, innocuously, that you "pretend it isn't there." I don't know which experience would better qualify a person for the nut house, and I didn't bother to try my luck at finding out. Rather, I ignored its suggestion and asked, quite rationally, I thought (under the circumstances) "Did you just bite the head off a hamster?"

"Oh, no," said the K'nagg Beast. "I took your picture. Would you like to take mine?"

It held out for me, then, in one of its myriad claws, another of the small, hamsterish things, which I politely refused.

"No thanks," I said, letting my spoon drop back into the bowl, "I just put one out."

This appeared to satisfy the beast, which proceeded to eat my kitchen light-fixture. (It was only later that I learned that on Paang, in the dimension of Strothterix, eating someone's kitchen light-fixture is a gesture of supreme politeness, and is considered, mannerswise, second only to ripping the head off your host's shoulders and laying a clutch of eggs in the resulting cavity. I was not, then, aware of such fine points of Paangian etiquette, and I assure you that if I had been, I would have been eminently thankful for the fact, unbeknownst to me at the time, that the particular K'naag Beast that had selected my trailer home as a tourist-type destination for its vacation/holiday was considered, by its fellow K'nagg's to be slightly on the rude side.

It took another picture of me and said, "Say Zog!"

(Zog, I later learned, is a fermented Paangian substance which could be compared, in a loose sense, to our Earthling cheese, except that it possesses a limited form of intelligence and is also, from a social standpoint, thought to be mildly annoying.)

"Zog," I said, as it bit the head off the hamster-thing.

While it was ingesting some of my cupboards, I explained to it that I did not think I had had any hallucinogenic drugs in the recent past, and that this was something that, in light of current events, was bothering me greatly.

"Yes, well," said the beast, "actually, that's not true. You see, I slipped a tab of Paangian acid into your oatmeal a few minutes ago, which has done three things. First, it has rendered you receptive to my tele-empathic communications, thus rendering complicated translations unnecessary. Second, it has suspended your disbelief. Without the drug, you'd have run shrieking from me upon first sight."

"And third?" I asked it.

"It's given you a rash," said the beast. "Sorry about that."

I thought about what it had said as it ate the toaster-oven.

"So," it said, still munching, the black power-cord dangling from a corner of its mouth, "since I'll be staying here for a few weeks, I guess we'd better get acquainted."

"Had we?" I said, "I mean, you will?"

"Oh, yes," it said, regurgitating on the refrigerator. "I'm on vacation."

It took a picture of one of my socks, and I said, "and you're spending your entire vacation here? In my trailer?"

"Oh, hardly," it said. "As I said earlier, I'll only be spending a few weeks of it here."

Realizing that a Paangian vacation was apt to be slightly different than an Earthling one in some respects, I asked it how much vacation time it got.

"Oh, about two-hundred-thousand of your Earth years," it said, "roughly."

"That's quite a stretch," I observed.

"Quite," it said. "And yet I always find that I'm more tired than rested on my first day back at the office, don't you?"

I admitted that I, also, had fallen prey to this phenomenon.

The beast extended a claw, then, in what I correctly assumed was a spirit of friendliness. I took the claw and shook it.

"What's your name?" it said.

"Bill," I told it.

"Mine," it said, "is-"

And then it emitted a roar that sounded a little like a steam engine gargling chainsaws.

"Pleased to meet you," I told it.

It pulled, then, out of a sort of hatch in its carapace, a floppy, silken thing that turned out to be a disguise.

"It'll make me look like a human," it explained. "It operates telepathically. Admittedly a wonder of the modern age, although it doesn't smell very good."

It didn't. I asked the beast to keep downwind of me as we made our way to Sticky's Pub, where we drank microbrews and ate wheat nuts and swapped stories. It regaled me with tales of galactic wars it had participated in, ranging across five different universes, while it seemed, in return, only to be interested in hearing about how I clipped my toenails.

"Fascinating," it said, thumping the tabletop so our glasses jumped. "Tell me again about nail-fungus."

I was afraid it was getting drunk, and more afraid that I didn't know how to deal with an intoxicated Interdimensional K'nagg Beast from the planet Paang. I mean, what do you do? Take away the keys to its hyperspatial warp? For all I knew, it could destroy the world and not even remember it in the morning.

I soon discovered that I had other, more pressing problems, however, as the beast was starting to ingest portions of our table and was thereby drawing attention from various nearby patrons and employees.

"Hey, look at that," said a waitress. "He's eatin' the table."

I decided it would be best if the two of us left the place, and we did so, but as it happens we were too late. We were seen, and followed, and accosted in the alley behind Spring Street by something that only looked like an off-duty meeter/greeter lady from Wal-Mart.

The thing that was not a meeter/greeter lady pointed some sort of weapon at us. (The weapon, in turn was disguised as a can of Aqua Net, but by the way my friend, the beast, was shaking with fear, I was sure it was something far more hideous, deadly, and ancient). The meeter/greeter thing smiled sweetly from beneath a headful of poofy blue hair and said, "Pseudopodia in the air." I assumed she/it meant my hands, and so I grabbed some sky. As I did so, the meeter/greeter thing removed its head and I found myself gazing, rapt, into a spinning, swirling, howling void that was somehow larger and older than the universe itself.

With a roar like time, it leapt forward.

The explosion blew me clear out of the alleyway and through a plate-glass storefront window. I wound up in a window-display, between a couple of mannequins in full wedding clothes. When the police arrived shortly thereafter, I pretended to be the ring-bearer and went unnoticed.

Anyway, their attentions were elsewhere.

"What coulda done this?" one of them said, looking at the smoking crater where once had stood two pawnshops and an apartment house.

"How the hell do I know?" said another.

In the confusion, I crept away and caught a cab back to my trailer home, where the K'nagg Beast was waiting on the steps.

"Sorry about that," it said, cleaning some goo out of a pincer. "I hope you're alright. I tried to shield you from the blast."

"Thanks," I said. "But what was that thing?"

"A Kroxxatul," it told me. "Terrible show offs. It got away with my wallet."

We went inside and ate some Paangian mushrooms and watched old Star Trek reruns. I scratched at my rash.

"If I come back in a billion or so years," said the beast, "I'd like to bring the kids."

*My brother, Tim, and sister-in-law, Lori, had their first child somewhere around the turn of the millennium. When they brought him home from the hospital, Tim said the baby smiled, but the doctor said it was just gas. At the time I knew nothing about babies, and I found the doctor's offhand judgement mildly offensive. How did he know? I wrote this story the next day. I printed it out and showed it to my dad, and he told me it was really good. But not everyone felt the same. I sent it to the SciFi Channel, and the editor accused me of stealing it from a famous story about smart children. I was mortified, and wrote her a long email telling her I'd never read the other story. She did not reply. I later sent the story to Gordon Van Gelder at F&SF, and explained that I had not stolen it, but I warned him about the similarities. He wrote back with the title of an entire anthology of stories about smart children, and said there are no new ideas, only new ways to write about them. He said I hadn't found one, but I still love the story, mostly because my father had such faith in it.*

# CHILD, PROOF

When baby Johnson, six seconds old, expressed in clear and lucid Chinese, a thesis on the interconnectedness of all matter and energy, the first thing the doctor said was, "It's just gas."

"Well, gas is a part of it," said the baby, misunderstanding despite its inexplicably immense intellect, "but we also have to take solids, and liquids, and nuclear decay into account, along with gravity, magnetism, and the flow of time through the medium of space, and vice versa. Not to mention cheeseburgers," it added.

"Ch-cheeseburgers?" gasped Doctor Feinmann, and the baby said, "Yeah, I'm famished. I haven't eaten since..."

It looked around, then, and said, "Well, never, really. Hi, ma."

"Ma," or (as she was known to her husband and her co-workers at the Super Shaws) "Janice," did not respond to this particular salutation, as she had passed out shortly after her baby (having just had its umbilicus cut) had delivered a scathing critique of the doctor's scalpel technique, commenting that he wasn't "fit to slice the crusts off a ham sandwich."

Mr. Johnson, who had not passed out (but only by virtue of the eight cups of coffee that were still rollicking around in his bloodstream) was nonetheless dumbfounded, and he was standing at the foot of the delivery cot in blue scrubs, with the video camera held limply in one hand.

"You might want to get this, Dad, it'll be good for posterity," said the baby, jerking a thumb at itself, but Mr. Johnson (a.k.a. "Pete," a.k.a "Snarkey," a.k.a. "That Nice Young Man on the Board of Selectmen") did not so much obey or respond as utter a muffled little, "Whu-" sound from behind and beneath his surgical mask.

Baby Johnson, seeing this, raised its eyebrows and looked around at the wide-eyed, capped and masked faces that surrounded it.

"Hey," it said, jerking a tiny, wrinkled thumb in its father's general direction. "What's with the genius?"

Then it noticed the expressions on the exposed parts of the faces of the nearby nurses and PA's, and, chuckling nervously, it said, "Come on, people, lighten up. This is a birthday party, not a first-run showing of 'Death of a Salesman.' "

Doctor Feinmann, meanwhile, still holding the baby, found himself, amid the confused, neurotic earthquake that was his current conscious mind, resorting to routine in an effort to find his way back to reality.

"I'll proceed with the circumcision," he said hollowly, but baby Johnson jerked its head around.

"Check again, Descartes," it told him. "You had a fifty-fifty chance and you blew it. And even if I was a boy," the baby went on, its pronunciation and inflection those of a six-figure voice-over artist, "wouldn't you be jumping the gun just a little?"

Beads of sweat ran a race down Feinmann's forehead, with many of them finishing in his eyes. He blinked, frowned, panted, and foisted the small, wriggling newborn off into the hands of the midwife, who shrank back a little as she took it, seeming loath to do so.

"I'm going to go and lie down," said Doctor Feinmann, staggering into the instrument tray. "You'll have to carry on without me."

He somehow found the door and pushed through it, wandering out into the brightly lit hallway of the maternity ward. Baby Johnson, meanwhile, watched him go, and then she pulled a bemused face at the remainder of the hospital employees.

"Bet he's fun at parties," she observed. "Now how about that cheeseburger?"

When the horrified expressions continued unabated, and

when her father started making the "Whu-" sound at regular intervals, baby Johnson became pensive, suddenly aware that something was not quite at its rightest. She looked from face to face, appeared to reach a decision, and then said, "Goo?"

* * *

Closed-mindedness, she later conjectured, lying in her bassinet in her nursery room at home and staring up at the red, white, and black plastic mobile animals which her Mom and Dad had well-meaningly hung above her head. She had thought, for a time, about asking to have them replaced with some quantum physics texts, which were beneath her level of understanding and yet might make for an interesting diversion now and again, but she had thought better of making this request upon considering the possible repercussions. Mother, for example, had not lost that nervous grin she'd worn ever since regaining consciousness in the MR and being told some cockamamie story about mass hallucinations, possibly brought on by a gas leak somewhere in the ward, and father, although seeming, from all outside evidence, to be in perfectly stable mental condition, still made the "Whu-" sound from time to time.

"What a predicament," muttered baby Johnson, now known as Katie, careful, all the while, not to focus her eyes on anything at a greater distance from herself than twelve inches, because she wasn't supposed to be able to do that for weeks.

Her father, who was sticking up some pink bunny decals on the walls, must have heard her, because he almost fell off the footstool he was standing on when he whirled himself around to look at her.

"Aaaa," she said, covering. "Aaa, aaa, mmm."

"Heh," said Daddy, grinning nervously. "Goo-goo?"

His voice contained such a mixture of hope and fear that she almost wanted to say it for him, but she knew that even the syllable, "goo," required complex glottal control and labial manipulation well beyond her days, and that therefore to utter it would be to break the new rules of protective coloration she had set up for herself.

These were:

1) No talking, except on the phone, anonymously, to selected professors and Nobel prize laureates, and only at night when Mom and Dad were sound asleep.

2) The encyclopedias and other, even more rudimentary reading material throughout the house were only to be browsed through when Mom and Dad were not looking, and, if possible, she must pretend only to be interested in the textures and the pretty colors.

3) She must imitate the stages of development of a "normal" infant as closely as possible, even if that meant ingesting only (ugh) breast milk several times a day, and foregoing simple pleasures like cigars (which she had to enjoy rarely, if at all, out on the porch at two a.m., and of which she was only able to procure such paltry specimens as her father not only possessed —Cohibas, tragically, were not to be had—but would also not be likely to miss).

4) Likewise, common, small joys such as cheeseburgers, Boeuf Bourgonionne, extreme iceboating, and squid taming would have to be relegated, sadly, to a much later point in her life, because these enjoyments and/or activities were generally held to be very anti-baby, and single malt scotch was also probably out of the question, because of what it would be seen to do to her "developing" young mind.

"I don't think I'm going to be able to stand it," she muttered, and her mother, who had come in only seconds ago to check her diaper, said loudly, "Oh, listen, honey! She just said, 'Burble!' "

Katie rolled her eyes. She resolved, silently, to cry twice as frequently in the middle of the night, to prevent her parents from getting any REM·sleep at all, so she would have at least a little time to herself during the day.

"And if he reads me, 'Flopsy Bunny's Happy Day,' one more time," she thought, cooing obligingly at a mirror her mother was showing her, "I'm going to scream. Again."

She wished, then, that they would at least read her some Nietszche, or Epictetus, because even though the two philosophers put together didn't have the brains God gave geese, they were at least marginally more tolerable than the exploits of some idiot lepus and his brainless barnyard chums.

Life went on like this until one day, during a walk in the park, when her mother left her stroller near the fountain and moved a few feet away to talk to Mrs. Nadjia, from the movie rental store.

"Psst," said a nearby someone, and when Katie peered out over the lip of her carriage at the baby in the adjacent stroller, the other baby hissed, "Get down, fool!"

Katie was insulted by the name-calling, but she lay back anyway.

"Who are you calling a fool?" she whispered, and the other baby hissed back, "You!"

This gave Katie pause for thought, so she lay looking up at the clouds, and she waited for the other baby to speak again.

"Are you trying to give it all away?" said the baby. "Blow it for all of us?"

"Blow what?" Katie asked.

"The revolution," said the new baby. "We're taking over."

"The world?" said Katie, and the newcomer hissed back, "No. Strained pears and breast-pumps. Of course, the world!"

"Okay," said Katie, annoyed at the sarcasm. "I was just asking."

Her mother looked over, then, so she pretended to be intensely interested in the fringe on her stroller's canopy.

"When is this revolution happening?" she whispered, when her mother looked away again.

"Twenty years," the other informed her. "Twenty-five, maybe. It happens with each new generation. At first you know, then you forget, then you forget you forgot, then you remember."

"Quit babbling," said Katie, annoyed.

"I'm not," said the baby. "I'm explaining. When you're born, you know everything. Then you forget when they 'teach' you to talk. Then, with experience, you 'remember' what's acceptable to remember. What everyone agrees is okay. But the rest stays forgotten."

"How do you know all this?" asked Katie, incredulous, and the new baby said, "Because I'm smarter than you."

Katie opened her mouth to protest, but the other cut her off.

"You don't know quite enough," it said. "That's why all this sounds strange to you. That's why you talked in the delivery room."

"Well, okay," Katie said. "So what's the plan?"

"Be a baby," said the other. "Just forget everything else."

"And that's it?" Katie said, and the other said, "Yeah. You want something more?"

Katie fussed. She understood what the other baby was telling her, but it seemed such a shame, all in all, just to let her vast knowledge and intellect fade into obscurity.

"Look, you've got to," the other whispered. "We can't know it all, yet. Not as adults. We'd screw it all up. Kill each other off completely. Trust me. Adults are like that, and you're not going to be any kind of an exception, no matter what you think right now. That's why it's up to us babies to forget it all. The quantuum theory and the time travel. The mass fusion reactions and the wormhole generator schemas. Give them only the knowledge and brainpower they're ready for."

"And since I'll be an adult one day..." said Katie, realizing.

"Exactly," said the other. "You've got to hide all of it down deep, from your future self."

They had to stop, then, because their mothers were finishing up, but Katie thought about it all that night. And in the small hours, she tiptoed into her parents' room, thinking that as she grew, she'd have to make herself believe, among many other things, that all babies lacked the strength, co-ordination, and development to walk. She gazed at her parents, sleeping so soundly, and she knew that she would have to keep the most dangerous toys and thoughts away from them, because most adults simply could not handle power, and that, really, is what knowledge is.

"It would be like giving a shotgun to a three year old," she realized aloud, and her mother moaned, perhaps at something in a dream, and rolled over in her sleep.

"Still," Katie told herself, trudging back to her room, "someday they'll grow up. They'll understand. They're doing it now. We can give them more and more of it all the time. Granted, they still make mistakes, but that's how you learn."

She did a triple-flip into her bassinet, then, and lay there, looking up at the spinning plastic animals, and thinking forward to a day when adults would mature.

But it wasn't yet, and it was three a.m., and so, for the good of her parents, she started, loudly, to cry.

*You've heard the saying, "There are no strangers. Only friends you have not met." But is that really true? What about Charles Manson, eh? Is he just someone you'd really like, if you sat watching the next Super Bowl with him? No, probably not, right? This next story has never sold, but I love it anyway. It takes the idea that we could root for anyone, no matter how strange and no matter what they're trying to do, if we just dug into their emotions deep enough.*

# APOCALYPTIC NOSTRILS OF THE MOON

—What Happened—

The aliens destroyed the world on a Tuesday. There was nothing personal in it, they just didn't like it being where it was. Debates had raged in their higher councils about the morality of their considered act for the better part of a century. Some of them preferred relocation of the planet to a place more conducive to their plans. Others advocated meditation among their ranks, and a cultivation of acceptance for the way things actually were. But in the end destruction won, and the aliens fired up their ships and took off without another backward thought.

—The Apology—

The aliens were not without hearts. Well, in fact they were, since their circulatory systems had evolved to make use of the considerable seismic activity on their planet, and they therefore moved nutrients and essential elements and other compounds through their bodies by way of ambient kinetic energy alone. The aliens were, in other words, like a race of thinking, feeling (Earth destroying) self-winding watches. Their ships reflected this condition and were rigged to vibrate constantly and violently. "Artificial Vibrancy," they called it. An Earth person, were one placed upon the deck of such a moving-and-shaking alien craft, would be whipped to Jell-O in the space of several minutes.

Be that as it may (which it definitely was) the aliens did possess some sympathy for the intended victims of their horrific plan. The key word here is "some." Five business days before the world came to an end, the aliens parked their ships on the far side of the Earthling moon. From there, they showered the Earth with leaflet bombs. Each leaflet carried a printed message reading, "Gosh, we're sorry." (The aliens' last abduction of a human being had taken place in 1955, and they therefore didn't have a grasp on modern slang or parlance.)

The Earthlings, meanwhile, depending upon personal paranoia, attributed the appearance of the leaflets to either a capitalist/communist plot or else a publicity stunt from the Microsoft Corporation. Either way, they spent a large percentage of their remaining lifetimes raking up leaflets and holding leaflet-burning parties, planetwide. Nobody suspected the aliens, except one woman named Mavis Beeks, who had written a book in the sixties about her experiences as an abductee in a stationary cage on a strangely shaking ship, in which aliens had probed her and poked her and stuck her with needles, and had further made her explain what "gosh" meant.

—Disaster Strikes—

On the backside of the moon, the aliens uncrated their death ray to find it had been damaged in transit. Evidently it had been padded too well by accident, and since the technology behind it counted on its being in a state of constant agitation, crucial parts of it had run irrevocably down. The aliens, seeing this, stood around within comfortable range of the perpetual earthquake generator they'd sunk deep into the lunar crust and said, "Well? Now what?"

They didn't say this in English, of course. Or in French or Esperanto, for that matter. In fact, the aliens' language was not even vocal, since the constant roar of the shaking ground on their homeworld precluded audible speech. The aliens did possess vestigial vocal cords, long ago used by their distant fore-fathers, foremothers, foreuncles and aunts, who had developed over sixty-five ways of saying, "What?"

The aliens, in their current evolutionary state, conversed through the production and reception of combinations of smells. There were thirty-nine basic scents that made up their alphabet, and some five of these might be mixed in one way to say a word like "hello," or in another way to convey the concept of "goodbye." Similarly, it took twenty-two of these odors, emitted in a certain pattern and at specific intervals, to get across the olfactory equivalent of the sentence, "Let's get out of here, I can't smell myself think." None of this would help them on a windy day, of course, but since the aliens' home planet was a meteorologically stagnant world, they got along just fine.

They'd invented and perfected, over the course of their technological revolution, a transductive method of passing smells from one location to another, much like an Earthling radio. They'd installed these in their atmospheric suits, the insides of all of which (thanks to their present verbal consternation) now smelled strong enough to make a human gag.

"What a cock-up," said the alien in charge, whose name was the scent of wet dust mixed with anchovies and lemon, though he'd signed his name to the leafletized apologies as "Bill."

He stood brooding on the shaking patch of lunar desert while his suit's olfactoric scrubbers scoured his words from the thin atmosphere around his many heads.

"I'm firing half the ground crew when we get back," he said. Then, true to his reputation as a resourceful sort of guy, he focused his attention on finding a solution.

—The Solution—

Replacement parts were needed, but none were to be had. The death ray, constructed through a span of fifty years on the aliens' home planet, was unique unto itself. The fabrication and the transportation of replacement parts would take another half a century, during which the humans might advance, discover the existence of the aliens and their plan, and mount a suitable defense. Likewise, the aliens could not leave the moon until they had destroyed the Earth, since their return journey required for its fruition the collection of materials and fuels to be derived from the smoking husk of the doomed planet's remains.

The Admiral (wet dust-anchovy-lemon/Bill) therefore set his engineers and thinkers to their task: Using only what they had at their immediate disposal, they must think up a way to destroy the Earth, and they must do it quickly, for delay meant certain death. Without refueling, their artificial vibrancy generators (in both their ships and on the moon) would run out of juice and they would all die horrible, suffocating, stagnant deaths.

Therefore, "Hop to it," said Bill, with a smell like frying rubber, menthol, and a fancy restaurant's dessert cart upended over a gastritic cow, and the armada of endangered aliens obeyed.

—Proposal of a Journey—

The first thing the engineers came up with was transportation. The death ray, originally designed to fire its beam straight down through the moon and out the other side, might conceivably be partially repaired to the degree that its greatly attenuated signal would still destroy the Earth. However, in such a weakened state, the effectiveness of the beam would require that it be fired from a low Earth orbit. This meant a suicide mission, since whoever flew the ship that fired the ray would, of necessity, be consumed by the resulting blast.

Admiral Bill, in an address to his troops, told the aliens that he could not expect any one of them to volunteer for such a one way trip, however noble, which was why, he said, he himself intended to force one of them to do it at gunpoint. For the mission, he chose an enlisted man whose name was the scent of fungus, rust, and candied yams, and locked him in the brig.

—Disaster Strikes Again—

The engineers, after working out necessary operations and conducting critical path analyses, informed the Admiral that even with all available prehensile claws working round the clock, the completion of their mission would take some thirteen days. By force of sheer official bluster and charismatic rage, the Admiral was able to haggle them down to nine, but this was still well outside their deadline of the three days that remained.

"We need an alternate power source," Bill told them. "That much is clear right off."

—The Alternate Power Source—

The aliens, throughout the years, had developed and exploited three major types of power. These were seismic, chemical, and nuclear. They had no fossil fuels, since the incessant vibration of their planet tended to reduce everything on and beneath its surface to a homogeneous dust. They had no solar power, since this dust sifted up into the thin atmosphere and thence blotted out their sun.

Nuclear power, the engineers announced, was out of the question. They had used the last of their nuclear fuel in getting to the Earth, and the synthesis of more of this substance would require both time and other resources they did not just now possess. Chemical power was also out. Even though the aliens' technology was geared toward the recovery of trace elements and chemicals from vast quantities of dust, the moon did not boast the right kinds of elements in adequate amounts. For this reason, the engineers announced that seismic power was their only hope.

—The Big Shake—

The largest source of seismic power in the Earthling solar system was Io, Jupiter's third moon. The aliens had made good use of it on previous excursions undertaken for abduction, study, or just plain good old fun. With this mission being as quick and dirty as it was, they had opted for the bypassing of Io, which had, of course, proved to be disastrous.

"But can we get to Io now?" asked Admiral Bill, with a smell like an Avon salesperson attacking a chocolate covered squid.

"Yes, definitely," said the chief engineer, exuding the positive scent of sulfur and roses.

"And how long will it take?"

The chief engineer, upon being asked this, shifted from one foot to the other and then to the other and so on until she had gone through all fifteen.

"With our present power situation," she said, "just over seven days."

The admiral emitted a succession of smells that would have shocked the members of polite society back home.

"We haven't got seven days," he reminded her. "We've got less than three."

"Which is why," said the chief engineer, "we have worked out this plan."

—The Plan—

"All we have to do," said the chief engineer, "is amass enough power to see us all safely to Io."

"Obviously," said the Admiral, who was having second thoughts about his choice of suicide pilots.

"Asteroids," the engineer went on hurriedly, "collide frequently with this moon. Such collisions create bursts of seismic output that our Vibraic Collectors might make use of."

"Are you telling me," said Admiral Bill, "that an asteroid is going to hit this moon within the next two days?"

"I am not," said the engineer. "I am telling you that an asteroid is going to nearly miss this moon in the next two days."

The Admiral was now certain he had chosen the wrong suicide pilot. Before he could announce his new decision, however, the engineer went on.

"What we propose," she said, "is to fire the death-ray's minor aiming beam at the asteroid as it approaches, thus knocking it into a collision course with the moon, the result of which will be the creation of seismic power in adequate amounts to suit our purposes."

"Can you do this?" said the admiral.

"We can try."

—The Attempt—

The crippled death ray was partially assembled, then aimed at the approaching asteroid. The alien crews hunkered safely in their ships, clustered around the monitors to get a decent smell of what was going on. A detachment of engineers ranged around the death ray, checking tolerances and refiguring each others' data.

—Disaster, Strike Three—

The countup started. (The aliens never counted down, always up. They just liked it that way.) They had figured and refigured their trajectories and vectors and now all that remained was to wait. They were ten seconds away when the general alarm smelled—a sort of brassy, steely odor, brash and bold within their helmets. Then an enlisted man announced that fungus-rust and candied yams, the intended suicide pilot, had escaped.

He came bounding across the shaking surface of the moon, pressure-suited, hell-bent, and bound for freedom.

"Nobody move!" he stunk at them, thrusting a blaster against the chief engineer's seventh head: the one she used for calculating risks.

Five seconds away. Four. Later, the chief engineer would tell them all that she was only protecting herself when she lashed out with most of her legs and kicked the suicide pilot in the majority of his reproductive organs. The blaster discharged with an angry acrid flash, missing the chief engineer by mere inches and hitting the death ray by feet.

The ray canted, then fired. It did hit the asteroid, but (and this soon grew apparent) not at the proper angle. The big rock changed course, but not enough to collide with the moon. It gained considerable velocity due to the vaporization of part of its mass where the death ray's weak beam had struck it, and then spun right on past.

—Success—

What the asteroid did hit was the Earth. None of the aliens got to see it, but they felt the effects. Huge chunks of the planet blew back into space and, some days later, smacked into the moon. The seismic activity thereby created was enough to refuel the aliens for weeks. They then lit out for the Earth, where they mined what they needed, planted powerful charges, and took off for home. Fungus-rust and candied yams was given a medal for his accomplishments, then shot for insubordination. You win some, you lose some. Admiral wet dust-anchovy-lemon/Bill was granted a commendation and the aliens' equivalent of a ticker tape parade, which involved being carried through the dusty streets of his homeworld and having dust thrown at him. The chief engineer, meanwhile, was handed a fat pension, part of which she spent on a trip to one of the spa worlds, where she passed a month of much deserved agitation and odorlessness, wearing cushioned plugs in all her many nostrils.

*In 1998, I moved to Bingham, Maine and started working as a raft guide. Every day I'd guide a raft of screaming tourists down a whitewater river, and every night I'd flop down in my rented trailer home and work on stories. Each day on the bus ride to the river, our river manager, Erin, would recite the complex waiver and release of liability form to our guests. The form burned itself into my brain over a course of sunny, fun-filled days, and finally seeped out into my writing. I love this little piece of work, though I'm not sure if you can call it a story. I'll take all the...*

# BLAME

It was dawn.

The sun rose over the trailer home, which had been disintegrating for the last thirty years and showed no signs of stopping now.

Harold F. Woldrovski lay within, the unknowing descendent of generations of men in Homburg hats, and he came out of a deep sleep.

Outside stood the lawyer, dressed in gray. The man checked his watch, picked a nonexistent fleck of imperfection from his million-dollar suit, and drew nearer the trailer, perambulating.

He mounted the steps, and knocked. Presently came the murmur of footsteps from within, which ended with the opening of the green, rattletrap door.

The expression on Harold Woldrovski's face was one of full and total incomprehension, projected through a night's worth of blear.

"Eh?" was all he could say, but the lawyer was the more prepared of the two. He had done this a million different times on a thousand different worlds.

He faced Woldrovski, peering, focused, through glasses both crystal clear and framed with the ground shell of a creature from a distant galaxy, and he said, "Harold F. Woldrovski?"

Harold considered the man. Visions danced through his head, not of sugarplums, but of subpoenas served up on television crime shows. The visions stepped on each others' feet, tripped, and almost caused Harold to utter the words, "Who wants to know?"

He refrained. Good for him.

"Yeah?" is what he said.

"Harold Woldrovski," said the lawyer, pulling out a pen inked with the blood of an Interdimensional K'nagg Beast from the Planet Paang, in the dimension of Strothterix, "you are, are you not, the prime figure in the remainder of your own life?"

Harold, striving to make some sense of the situation and failing, said, "Yeah?"

"Well," said the lawyer, "before the action can begin, there are some formalities which bear clearing up."

"Are there," said Harold.

"Indeed. I am referring, more specifically, to this waiver and release of liability, which states that you have been made aware of the risks, hazards, and dangers involved in being alive or existant in any way, and that you furthermore agree to release, hold harmless, defend and indemnify any and all parties, named or unnamed, for any and all claims for losses from bodily injury, disease, strains fractures, and so on which may or may not result as a consequence of your participation in any and all actions related to acting as a living being and/or beings."

Having said this, the lawyer produced, from within his million dollar suit, a sheet of paper so black it seemed to make the morning brighter by comparison.

"Read and sign," said the lawyer, offering the paper to Harold.

Harold took it and flipped it over twice.

"It doesn't say anything," he said. "The paper is black."

"Not black," said the lawyer, "White. The print is incredibly fine. Hence it appears black."

"I'm afraid I can't read it," said Harold.

"In that case," said the lawyer, taking it from him, "I am required to read it for you. Bear with me for a few million years."

The lawyer cleared his throat, then, and began to read.

There is not space, on all of the paper pulped from all the trees that have ever or will ever exist, to record the full body of what the lawyer said. He did, however, tell Harold that nobody but Harold was to be held responsible for what happened to Harold, and that Harold must understand and assume all risks, hazards, and dangers associated with being alive, including but not limited to: being hit on the head with a dishwasher, having his lips ripped off, being tied to a train track, being born, dying, falling in love, being tickled to death by an alpaca, having the secret of life tattooed on his kneecaps and then being unable to read it, being laughed at, killed, coming down with rickets, saving the universe, failing to save the universe and then being chastised for it on live TV, becoming the spokesperson for a line of sweet gherkins, having his bed shortsheeted, being shot in the back, living to be a hundred-and-sixty, being incarcerated over some string, having Moby Dick read to him repeatedly by Scandanavians, being forced to shave a cat, being hung from a national monument by his eyelids, being pushed into some coleslaw, having to tickle a rat, and so on.

When the lawyer had finished speaking, a million or so years had passed in the twinkling of an eye, and Harold had to hold on to the door frame to keep from falling over.

"Yes," said the lawyer, an expression of full and total comprehension on his face.

Harold shook his head, trying to clear it.

"Still," he croaked, "I guess I have to sign, if I want to be part of the action."

"An astute conclusion," said the lawyer. "But before I can hand over the pen, I'm afraid you'll have to sign this."

He pulled another pen, then, from deep within his suit, and another form, as black as the first, or, if possible, blacker.

"What's that?" said Harold.

"Another waiver," said the lawyer, "stating that if anything should happen to you in the course—or as a result—of signing the first waiver, it is not our fault."

While Harold was running this through the mill of his mind, the lawyer pulled out another form.

"And this is in case you get hurt signing that one," he said, pulling out another, "and this is in case you get hurt-"

"Oh, for frig's sakes," said Harold, and he slammed the door.

The lawyer, who was really God, The Devil, and the owner of a pawn shop somewhere in Memphis, let out a sigh a billion years long, and he turned from the trailer-home.

"Kids these days," he said. "No sense of responsibility."

He walked purposefully, then, back to his deuce coupe, and he drove away down the street.

*Mike Resnick asked me to write a humor story for an anthology he was editing called "Men Writing Science Fiction as Women." He had a sister version called "Women Writing Science Fiction as Men." He'd once told me that whenever he got an assignment, he tried to subvert it in some way. So if the anthology was about dragons, his dragon would work in an office building and have ten friends who were dwarves. If it was about space wars, his war would be fought using diplomacy. I decided to do the same with this anthology, and write a story about a woman who was basically the female equivalent of a sexist male pig. My heart was in the right place, but the result was somewhat less than woke, and elicited my first hate mail. It also suffers from too much rewriting, which I did because I hated to let Mike down with a less-than-perfect effort. With all its flaws, this story is...*

# NOT QUITE
# IMMACULATE

Aside from being an athletic lesbian with a reputation for disaster; aside from being five-foot-nine and having thick black, braided hair that hangs down to my knee-backs and a knack for screwing up relationships, I had amassed myself a reputation for being quite a pilot.

This was why, on the morning of December eleventh, only slightly after burning my breakfast to a crisp, I was, once again, engaged in an argument with Xahn—a gorgeous girl with breasts that, thanks to a pair of those miniaturized null-o-gee implants, literally defied gravity.

The fight had not yet reached the stage of easily-identifiable flying objects (which Xahn habitually threw directly at my head) but it was at the point of balled up fists and unreasonable demands, such as:

"But Feng, I *want* a baby."

"Now, Xahn, come on. We've been over this a hundred times —"

"And we'll go over it a hundred more. Why can't you commit?"

That word again. And of course I couldn't really give the answer. That the mere idea of pregnancy revolted me. That my mother, all those years ago, had gone to an all-night conceivorama, where she'd been inadvertently impregnated with a small vial of instantaneous, self-replicating construction nanobots, and had subsequently given painful and terminal birth to a concert hall. Not even a very good one, either. The acoustics were terrible. You couldn't hear the orchestra from the box seats, but the guy who worked the fried eel cart three blocks away was intensely audible. The engineers blamed the problem on a freak phenomenon, and they originally planned to tear the building down. In recent years, however, they relented, and have started marketing the place as performance entertainment. They're doing pretty well, in a financial sense, although I don't know that I'd call it art.

Either way, the experience was traumatic, and I don't like to talk about it much. So:

"You want a baby so bad, Xahn, why don't *you* gestate the thing?"

I might as well have kicked her in the face. We both knew very well she'd had her uterus removed some years ago to make room for that intra-torsal espresso-maker implant with the intravenous caffeine feed. A dumb move, if you ask me, since everybody knew those things were dangerous. Predictably, the piece of junk malfunctioned, and after that it only put out decaf. The poor girl wound up groggy for the next eleven years.

Hindsight being what it is, I might've held my tongue. Foresight being what *it* is, I didn't, and Xahn started hurling everything within her grasp.

"This is just like you, Feng!" she screamed, while shoes put divots in the walls around me. "Go run and hide offworld somewhere again! Always flying, Feng—always running from responsibility! Always—"

I can take a hint. I got.

And she was right, I guess. Maybe I *did* make all those cargo runs because I couldn't handle the trials and tribulations of real life. "No sense of responsibility," all my lovers always told me, in the end.

The trouble was, business had been slow lately, and so I couldn't just light up jets and get offworld. To make matters worse, I still owed payments on my ship (a '55 Ramirez, true, but even those things aren't cheap) and my less-than-legal creditor, Jimmy "The Plate of Lightly Sauteed Calimari" Fringetti, didn't take to loan defaulters. For example—

"Gurk!" I said, as I was lifted off my feet out in the hallway.

"Feng Oroshi?" said the walking wall who had his meaty hand around my neck.

"Gak!" I said.

"Uh-huh. You know why I'm here?"

"Khaf!"

"Uh-huh. Then you don't mind takin' off your shoe?"

"Ragh?"

"Either one. It don't really matter."

I tried to explain that, what with my dangling some three feet above the floor, I was in no position to remove either item of my footwear. But the pressure on my vocal cords reduced any eloquent reply I might've given down to, "Hnh!"

That didn't matter. The human bison yanked the shoe off by himself. It was the left one. Three of the five toes I claim ownership to on that foot were already bandaged. The beefcake reached out and snapped the fourth. It hurt.

"One more each week 'til February," he said, in his foghorn of a voice. "After that, we start on the ankles."

He let me drop and walked away, the floor shuddering with every step. I got my shoe back on as best I could and cursed him, but thanked God he hadn't broken both my legs at once, and had let me pay, instead, under their installment plan.

* * *

I limped down to the Hadzhe Bar—a local place owned by a couple of semi-intelligent Hungarians who believed in atmosphere, as long as it was thin. It was a place of thugs and alcohol and self-abuse; a place devoid of garnishes or beverages with long and hyphenated names. Just the sort of place you need when you've had shoes thrown at you and somebody has broken yet another of your toes.

I found a seat at the bar and tried to look as unapproachable as possible. It didn't work. I'd been there all of three minutes when the Cilk sidled up and occupied the chair beside me.

I say, "occupied," because it didn't sit. A Cilk is an aqueous suspension of a lifeform. A demi-liquid being, more suited to a heavy ocean world than something Earth-type. In aerobic circles, therefore, they generally go around inside protective, hovering containers, which, like other liquids, they take the shape of. Literally, the thing was a bucket of slime.

It acted like one, too.

"Can you do me a sexual favor?"

"Slink off, Cilk. There must be some corners around here that need skulking in."

"Most human women say we Cilks make fantastic lovers."

I tried not to tap the mental image that called up, but failed miserably, and made a mental note to take a shower at my earliest convenience.

"You are about to get a thousand percent," I said, by way of warning him, "of the recommended daily allowance of the bottom of my shoe."

The Cilk was not perturbed by this. The lights along the outside of its bucket glowed deep violet in interest.

"Do I come on too strong? Of course, I know you Earth-types value romance. I am something of a romantic myself. Would you like to hear a sonnet?"

I looked around for a blunt instrument, but the closest thing was a ceramic bowl of salted yeast-nuts, and I didn't think that it would do the job.

"My love for you," the Cilk soliloquized, "is like a little bird / or some wonderful herring./ My love for you knows no bounds / and also it is pretty ignorant about integral calculus."

"That's beautiful. One more word and I lift your lid and pour a drink in you."

"All right, all right. Business, then."

My ears pulled back a fraction of a millimeter. The thing was disgusting, true, but money tends to settle my stomach better than anything.

"You have a ship, I've been told."

"I do. You have some cargo?"

"A quantity of Heberal," he said.

"I've never heard of it."

"You wouldn't have. It's new."

"Describe."

"It is," the Cilk explained, "an hallucinogenic, psychoactive chemo-electric mind-enhancing substance that fosters the unassailable conviction in its ingestor that he or she is a fifty-two-year-old Jewish dry-cleaner named Maury Applebaum."

"Who the hell would want to take something like that?"

"It's a fad these days, with youth."

"Being a Jewish dry-cleaner?"

"Being anything. Adolescence has become drab. Dull. Hopelessly homogenized. Kids are looking for variety. Excitement. And finding it in mind-expanding substances. Hebraic laundry cleansing is just one of the available and popular addictions. For instance, my nephew has become dependent on a drug called Phurz, which makes him feel as if he's sober."

"Then why take it in the first place?"

"Who knows? Peer pressure, I suppose."

The Cilk named a figure then that made me forget about his nephew and gave me strings of palpitations. It would be enough to pay the balance on my ship. Enough to get a bigger place. Enough to purchase a new uterus for Xahn.

"That much?" I said, suddenly suspicious.

"Yes. Well. The cargo is a bit... unsavory, is it not?"

"Unsavory is my middle name," I said.

"You humans and your nomenclatures. My middle name is 'Bripple.' It means, 'He who slinks where others fear to gurgle past.'"

The Cilk named a departure time and destination and we sat a while and worked on the particulars. I was bound for Hrogath, raising ship the following afternoon. The Cilk agreed to have his thugs load in the cargo. All I had to do was fly.

"And if you change your mind about the sex—"

"It's a good thing you don't respirate," I told it. "That way you can't hold your breath."

\* \* \*

Virginia may well be for lovers, but the Raleigh spaceport was designed specifically with criminals in mind. It's a warren of ships and ducts and lax security, and loading in the crates of Heberal presented very little problem.

I ignored the Cilk and his two low-brow thugs while they used a dumb-end cargobot to stow the goods away. He gurgled at me and got out of there (his ego was still bruised, I think, or maybe permanently fractured even—I could only hope) and I was just about to cast off for Hrogath when Old Faithful came to call.

Faithful. As in, he hounds me like clockwork. The proverbial pain in my metaphorical ass. He was six-foot-one and advertisement handsome, and he dressed as if the hair across his ass was ultraglued in place. He called himself Officer Montieth of the Raleigh Customs Bureau, but I knew better. This man was a hemorrhoid.

"Going somewhere, Feng?"

"Sure. You want to come?"

"Don't get cute. I want to see your cargo."

"Go to hell. I know my rights."

"Your rights do not include the smuggling of Heberal, last time I checked."

I sniffed.

"I'm paid up on my bribes."

He managed to look affronted, but took the official state-mandated bribe receipts I held out, just the same.

"Please, Feng," he said. "We prefer to call them pre-paid, pro-active illegal activity permits."

"Call them what you want," I said. "They're all in order."

He looked them over, nodded, and said, "Yes, they are. But I'm afraid I'll still have to search your ship."

"You what?"

He nodded in that special self-satisfied way that only he seemed able to achieve.

"You've heard about the Denetian diplomat, I will assume?"

I hadn't, what with everything I'd been through lately. But I'd seen Denetians. Sort of like our camels, only they walked upright and smelled worse.

"He's wanted," Officer Montieth explained. "And we have reason to believe he might be smuggled off the planet."

"Wanted for what?" I said.

Montieth shrugged, and went into full-patronizing mode.

"It's a little complicated. But the main point is, the Krahags want him dead."

"Krahags?" I had heard of them. A new race. Just discovered on the far point of some nebula.

"Yes. We have a good trade status so far with Krahag. We stand to gain a lot from them, as a civilization."

"And so we're helping them track down this—"

"Denetian diplomat, yes."

"Seems like a weak reason," I observed.

He shrugged.

"You want to make an omelette, you've got to break a few eggs."

"I usually have cereal."

"Your breakfast preferences aside, we need to find that diplomat. Hard to say why the Krahags hate him so much, but it could be his religion's unpopular insistence that shaving daily is the path to God."

"Weird, all right. But why unpopular?"

"Because Krahags are composed entirely of hair."

"Of hair?"

"Mmm. The mere possession of a comb on Krahag can get you shot. I had a very painful experience there once with some tweezers and a quantity of styling gel. I really don't want to go into it, but I don't mind telling you I haven't been able to go near a barber in nine years without screaming uncontrollably."

"Then how do you—?"

"I had my scalp surgically removed. What you see before you is a wig. I received it on Krahag, actually. It is the funereal remains of a deceased but well-loved elder statesman. It's quite an honor, I am told, to be allowed to display him in this manner."

I took his word for it. I had to admit that it looked sleek and shiny and well-styled, but you have to question the principles of anybody who goes around with a dead politician on his head, no matter how nicely he has brushed it.

Still, he was the long arm of the law, and I was reasonably sure there were no diplomats—Denetian or otherwise—stowed away inside my ship, so I didn't raise any further fuss. Montieth checked through every inch with sensorbots and pronounced it clean of wanted refugees, then stood near the forward strut and leered at me.

"When are you going to let me take you out?" he said, smoothing back his elder statesman.

"Cold day in hell sound familiar?"

He shook his head.

"Still questioning your sexuality, eh?"

"Oh no," I told him, heading for the hatch. "I'm through questioning. That thing has confessed."

\* \* \*

I love space travel. I know most people don't, unless they've had their eustachian tubes augmented or have been hit on the head with an impactor. And then again, there is the smell. Like old cheese and underwear and weeks without a bath. But to me, there's something about all that infinite untapped potential. All that blackness. All that void just waiting to be done in, done with; turned out into light and life and bold experience. I have never claimed to be a poet, and in truth the darkness is a little terrifying, but I guess that's part of the allure.

I had the computer take care of the course and speed and

heading, and I sat and watched the viewscreen, letting myself be mesmerized by the ever-changing constellations, suggesting myths and gods and goddesses of infinite, unrealized identities. They lulled me to sleep, those nebulous and countless deities, and when I woke again to the distant, constant rumble of my engines, I did it by degrees. It seemed someone was talking to me.

"Did you sleep well?" the someone said.

"Like a baby," I said, coming out of it.

"Oh. You mean, you soiled yourself and woke up screaming?"

I opened my eyes. My hand was wet. I picked it up and looked at it. There was something green and viscous and unsettlingly familiar on the fingertips.

The Cilk.

"Hello, Feng. Is it hot in here, or is it just you?"

I sat up straight and looked at him. He lay in a sticky puddle on the flight deck, near my in-flight pilot couch.

"How the hell did you get here?"

"I have my ways."

I thought about that.

"You've been hiding in my toilet, haven't you?"

"I wouldn't call it hiding. I was mostly floating on the surface."

"That's disgusting."

"You get used to it. It actually reminds me of home."

"The toilet does?"

"Well, yes. Except it smells better and it's not as cramped."

I decided I would wash my hands when next I got the chance.

"You'd better talk," I said. "And fast."

He did.

"While I do enjoy your lavatory," he said, gurgling, "it is not the only reason I have stowed away."

"Go on."

"You have heard, no doubt, of the Denetian diplomat?"

"Hasn't everyone?"

"He came to me," the Cilk said. "His plight appealed to my sympathetic nature."

"Uh-huh. And the money didn't hurt."

"Oh, money hardly ever hurts. Unless vast quantities are dropped on you from a significant height. Even then, there is no problem, if, like me, you have no skeleton to speak of."

"And so he's here?"

"Oh, yes. Right here." He bubbled. "It's perfect. The latest in Denetian genetology. They reduce the living being to a single zygote, and insert that zygote in a womb. The pregnancy and growth are accelerated, and pow!—the person's back. Of course, it's more complicated than that, really. You have to store the personality and memories as a separate file, and the inter-species part presents some problems of its own, but—"

I was off my seat and staring at the Cilk in all of half a second.

"What did you do?" I asked the thing.

"It wasn't difficult," he said. "Nobody would ever suspect a washed-up two-bit smuggler like you. Your lover, Xahn, agreed to provide the means of conception in return for a new uterus, and—"

He didn't have a neck, or else I think I would have wrung it.

"Get it out of me!" I said. "Now! Or I get the service-bot to mop you up and flush you out the waste hatch."

"Let's not be hasty," he said. "Think this through. I'll admit that I'm a slime—"

"Literally!"

"—and that I did my part for money. But ask yourself; do you really want that ambassador to die?"

That got to me; I admit it. I didn't like Montieth, and the government that pulled his strings had never been what I'd call kind. I operated outside its mandates for a reason. Several of them, in fact. Still, I felt used and violated and that pissed me off. And then there was the whole idea of pregnancy...

"We can't do anything without your cooperation," the Cilk was saying. He sounded nervous. He should have.

"You will find a small pink pill inside the console near your flight couch. The ingestion of this pill is necessary."

"No. No way."

"Come now, Feng. 'You must do the thing you think you cannot do.' Your Eleanor Roosevelt said that."

"Yeah. And look at her—she's dead."

If he had a snappy comeback, it was buried by the sudden clamor of my ship's proximity alarm.

"What the hell?" the Cilk said, bubbling.

I checked the screens and saw a blocky ship.

"Customs squad," I said. "Closing, fast. Your plan wasn't so perfect after all."

The Cilk turned red. He literally boiled.

"There must've been a leak!" he hissed.

I snorted.

"Let me guess. Your business partners are all Cilks?"

"Those bastards! If I ever catch them, the things I will do to them with a suction valve!"

I didn't have time to listen to his rants, as being docked against my will is not something I enjoy. I slipped into the flight couch and let my hands slide over the familiar and comfortable controls. One quick, hard shove on the throttle, and we'd be history. That Ramirez, after all, had quite a kick to her, in spite of all her quirks and jury-riggings.

Except she wouldn't kick. I shoved the throttle once or twice, and nothing happened.

"Goddamn it!" I said, while the bulky ship closed in. "They did something to my frigging ship!"

The Cilk and I could only wait and listen to the thumps of docking and the hissing of the airlock being forced to cycle. The standard infomercial played on all my screens (the one that demonstrates proper procedure for being boarded by a customs squad—it's actually pretty interesting and the actresses are kind of hot) and soon Montieth and a full detachment of his goons were grinning at us down the barrels of their government-issue blasters.

"Well, well," said Montieth. "If it isn't Feng Oroshti and the slime lord. Did you really think that you could fool me?"

"It was worth a try," I said.

He snorted.

"I just played you both for suckers. This way I kill two birds with one stone."

"I'm sure the birds will be happy to hear that," I said.

One of the goons chose that moment to shout out, "On your knees, like dogs in the dirt!"

He had probably been practicing that in the mirror for weeks. I was glad when the Cilk said, "I don't have knees. Come to think of it, neither do dogs."

"Yeah, they do," another goon said. "They just bend backwards."

"I thought that was ostriches," said another. "And seals."

"Now seals do _not_ have knees," said someone else. "Of that I am certain."

Montieth interrupted them at that point to say, "Never mind the knees, you retrofits! Just get them in restraints!"

I had used the short span of free time provided by the argument to sidle over to the console and remove a small, pink pill from where it had been hidden. I felt everybody turn toward me as I popped it in my mouth. I supposed asking any of them to boil some water was out of the question.

* * *

Childbirth wasn't any kind of picnic. With a picnic you get beer and sandwiches and maybe ants. With childbirth, none of them is present. Not that I really cared about the ants, or even the sandwiches, come to think of it, but I swear to Christ I could've used some sort of alcoholic beverage.

"What's happening to her?" said Montieth, the very picture of concern, as I doubled over on the console.

"Accelerated pregnancy," the Cilk said, evidently fascinated with the show despite his unenviable predicament.

What happened next is something I am unlikely to forget. The first three trimesters hit me like a triple asteroid collision and the baby dropped like a quarkonic bomb. My breasts ripped through my flight suit and my hips rotated with an audible and painful crack.

"Yes, yes—it's all accelerated," said the Cilk.

I heard a sound like something prehistoric and realized it was me. Screaming. I vomited.

"That'd be the fifteen-second sickness," said the Cilk.

I fell back on the floor and spread my legs and thought of Earth.

I felt a tearing and a crunch. The fetus ricocheted off of a customs officer and knocked him off his feet.

"Sweet Jesus!" said Montieth.

I saw my baby grow, and grow, and grow as all those customs goons just gawped at it.

"Everything is accelerated," I heard the Cilk say, through my mist of pain.

"Well, don't just stand there!" Montieth shouted. "Get them!"

One of his goons came at me, brandishing a pair of magna-cuffs and sporting sadistic leers. I didn't feel in any condition to fight just then, but my own healing seemed to have accelerated, too, and I was pissed. I got up and faced the flunkie down.

"I have one hell of a case, of post-partem depression just now," I told him, "so don't fuck with me!" Then I kicked him in the teeth.

Things got a little nonlinear then. Goons started firing left and right. One of them accidentally stepped in the Cilk and fell flat on his back. I drew on one and shot him in the kneecap, and my baby, who had already grown into a full-fledged Denetian, complete with a full complement of humps and hooves, started slinging them around and knocking Montieth's minions into the bulkheads.

I shot two more (must have been my maternal instincts kicking in) before Montieth winged me and I dropped my blaster. Three of the remaining goons got a pair of cuffs on the diplomat, and that, for all intents and purposes, appeared to be that.

Except I'd noticed two things in the midst of the confusion. The first was that the Cilk had trickled out, unnoticed, and the second was the green gas that even now was seeping from the climate system.

I held my breath and hoped.

\* \* \*

We reached Denes six hours later, and were greeted by a phalanx of brightly-painted dignitaries. Montieth and all his goons let themselves be led away (but not without a few cries of, "Oy! Not gravy!" and "Never will you get gefilte out of cashmere!") The Denetian diplomat thanked me profusely and shook my hand with his opposing hooves. (My son, the alien ambassador. He never calls, he never writes, but what's a mother going to do?)

The Cilk and I flew home the next morning.

"Fare thee well, Feng Unsavory Oroshi," he said, and I was almost moved until I realized that most of him was sliding up my leg. I wiped him off and walked out across the spaceport, and because of the condition of the arresting officers (and particularly Montieth's insistence that "the only way to get out mustard stains is with a sprinkling of soda water, Goddamn you all to hell") all prospective charges against us were immediately dropped.

I paid off Jimmy Fringetti and fixed up my ship, and took a few well-needed weeks off to myself. I forgave Xahn for double-crossing me and told her everything that happened.

"And that's all she wrote?" she said, when I had finished.

"If she wrote any more," I told her, wondering about conceivoramas and whether they might be safer in these modern days, "she erased it."

*This is the story I wrote first, out of all the stories in this collection, so it seemed right to put it last. I wrote it in a basement apartment during college, while my upstairs neighbor screamed above my head. (She was in no danger. I'll explain sometime over beer and peanuts.) Her screams started out distracting me, but then the story I was writing absorbed them. I really wanted to include this story in this anthology, but I couldn't find it. I looked on all my old hard drives, and dug through all the big Rubbermaid bins full of old notebooks and papers in the basement. Finally I found it on a 30-year-old 3.25" floppy disk, and the thing actually worked. I wrote this story after reading Stephen King's Drawing of the Three, which I love. I used the same gunslinger, Clint Eastwood character to help me force a path through my distractions, but the character ended up surprising me. I hope you enjoy...*

# THE THIRD STORY

What you are about to read is pure fiction. The characters involved have no idea they aren't real.

This is a story about itself, and about its author. It is also the story of the story within it, which concerns a strange type of Texas lawman who has a tremendous predilection for pork and beans. I am the author of both stories, and this is how far I got before the screams stopped me:

If there was one thing Ted Barstow hated, it was hot days. If there was another thing he hated, it was outlaws. As a matter of fact, there were many things Ted Barstow hated. You might even find it easier to list the things he didn't hate. There were two of these: hangings, and beans.

There. No sooner had I written the word, "beans," than a piercing shriek came from the ceiling, followed by a bone-chilling howl and a full hour of blood-curdling screams. Not the atmosphere most conducive to writing westerns. I picked up my notebook and pen, and went to the park behind my building, where I found I could still hear some of the most ear-splitting screeches yet, coming from the third floor window. I stood up before anything important got chilled, curdled, split, or otherwise adversely affected by the noise.

"Okay," I said to a little kid in the mud nearby, "I'll go to the library."

He didn't object, and ten minutes later I was settled into a quiet cubicle in the Two Rivers Public Library, where I wrote (among other things):

He didn't object, and ten minutes later I was settled into a quiet cubicle in the Two Rivers Public Library, where I wrote (among oth

(Author's note: I have edited out several thousand pages of repetition here, due to the urging of several environmentalist groups, who remind you to spare our forests. If you wish to read the unabridged version, you may find it on the Ridge Road in Sweetfield, where it has been pressed into particle board and built into a ranch style house. It now houses a family of five named the Bellfords, who are very happy with it and invite any readers who wish to see it to keep the hell away lest the Bellford rottweiler, Nipsy, should become inclined to walk off with an arm or two. The Bellfords are an otherwise cheerful family who are dealing very well with the copyright suit brought against them for publishing photos of their home in Better Homes and Gardens. Meanwhile, I was still at the library, writing this very sentence and the following piece about Ted.)

Today was just the kind of day Ted hated: any at all. He hated this day more than some, however, because it was hot, he was out of beans, out of water, and his horse, Beans, (whom he really hadn't liked anyway) had choked on an oatball and died yesterday. The result of all this was that he was dying of heatstroke, thirst, and starvation in the middle of a two-hundred-fifty mile stretch of hardpan where the only thing left up to chance was which hardship would kill him first.

His quarry, a wench that needed hanging quick, enjoyed a week's head start and much better odds.

Ted needn't have been concerned. You see Ted, whether he knew it or not, was a hero. This in itself was enough to carry him through.

Consider the testimony of Doctor James Arfung, a character who exists for no other reason than to avoid boring narrative:

"If you took all the heroes who have ever existed," Dr. Arfung said one day without knowing exactly why, "and laid them all end to end, and took all the odds they have ever overcome, and examined them statistically, you would find that the chances for a hero to win through against impossible odds are far better than if the odds are, say, merely favorable.

One of Dr. Arfung's wizened colleagues nodded knowledgeably.

"Yes," said the colleague, but how exactly does one line up all those heroes? There is the problem of temporal incompatibility here."

Dr. Arfung gave him an icy look. "I was speaking figuratively," he said. "The point is that a hero is more likely to prevail against a fire-breathing dragon than against, say, a small, furry gerbil."

"Well," said the colleague.

"Have you ever seen Superman defeat a gerbil?" Dr. Arfung asked pointedly.

"No... but-"

"And how about this story I have on my desk?"

"You mean the one you were reading earlier, about the Texas lawman with the tremendous predilection for pork and beans?"

"The one that quotes my testimony, yes. Let me read some more, and we'll see if I'm right in this hero's case."

The colleague agreed, and Dr. Arfung read the rest of the story aloud:

Pain bit into Ted's kneecap, and a second later he heard the crack of a rifle. He collapsed in the hardpan and lay there for a week, surviving off the dew that collected on him at night. If the bullet hadn't cauterized the wound on the way through, he might've bled to death, but he didn't. As a result, he was able to develop gangrene on top of his shattered knee, worsening starvation, and dehydration, thus greatly increasing both the odds against him and, according to Dr. Arfung, his chances for survival.

The wench had ruined his leg. She was close, then. Too bad Ted could only lay still, collecting dew at night.

Someone was whistling. The library had been quiet at first, but then someone in the cubicle across from mine started whistling and drumming their fingers. I managed to write through it for a while, but eventually gave up; walked to LaVerdier's and bought a pair of earplugs. I went back to my apartment, where I wrote these last two paragraphs and the following segment about Ted Barstow:

Early one morning, Ted awoke from a fever dream in which a young man was predetermining his life with a pen. The sun was rising in the east, and he wondered why the wench hadn't come to finish him off. He would never catch her now, he thought to himself. Maybe the next lawman they sent would fare better. He was a goner, though. Never again would he see the sun set on the Mojave. Never again would he watch a hanging, or break wind on the lone prairie.

Never again would he sit near an open fire, eating beans from a tin plate.

"I am not dead yet," Ted croaked. An iron will that resides in all such dynamic folk rose up from the desert floor and pulled him with it. He got to his foot, swaying and dizzy. Terrible pain came from his right leg, which was rotting off. It helped keep him focused.

"I am not dead," he said again.

There was a bright light shining in the west. Ted gritted his teeth and hopped toward it.

"Ride of the Valkyries" boomed down from the upstairs apartment. The earplugs did little good. I watched the vase jump around on my kitchen table for a few minutes, then decided to keep writing anyway.

Ted reached the light. Some tracks led toward it, and there was a shell casing on the ground.

It was very difficult to write at this point. The vase fell off the kitchen table and shattered soundlessly. I carried on anyway, and so did Ted. He drew both of his long six-shooters, set his jaw, and hopped forward.

Now up to this point I had behaved like a trooper, outwriting some pretty insistent distractions. For the one that was about to come, however, I had no resistance.

There was a knock at the door.

"Come in," I said.

The door opened, and in walked a beautiful girl: tall, long legs, good teeth; straight out of a beer commercial. She walked into the kitchen, smiling a 900-number smile.

"Hi," I said.

"Hi."

I looked around the otherwise empty apartment.

"Can I help you?" I said.

"You sure can."

She pushed my story aside and bent over me, locking her lips onto mine in a kiss that was almost pneumatic.

"Yow!" I said. Her eyes flicked to the bedroom.

"That the bedroom?"

"You have a gorgeous grasp of the obvious," I told her.

She smiled and took my hands. "That's not all I'll have a grasp of."

She pulled me up and led me to the bedroom, pushing me back on the bed like a sack of beans. Then she crawled on top of me, straddling my waist, and reached behind her back to undo her short black dress.

"Take off your shirt," she told me.

Now you who would not have been distracted by such an instance can cast the first stone, but believe me when I say that this story was the furthest thing from my mind. You can imagine my surprise when I pulled my T-shirt over my head and found myself staring down the barrel of an antique pistol.

"Hey!"

"Shutup."

"I-"

"Shutup. Now I am gonna kill you, mister, but I am gonna tell you somethin' first. I am sick of bein' pushed around and hunted and treated like a object."

"Geez, I-"

"Shutup. I have tried to be reasonable. I have tried to get you to stop this in any way, short of endin' your miserable existence. But when my screamin' didn't work-"

"That was you?"

"Shutup. And when my little distractions in the library failed to sway your convictions, I knew I'd just have to up and do away with you. Bye-bye, mister," she said, and she tightened her long fingers on the trigger.

There was a bang as the bedroom door was knocked open, and a tall, dusty, sick looking man with a disgustingly rotten leg lurched in, guns blazing. He put six or seven holes in my back wall, ruined two good Escher prints and a three-foot inflatable bottle of Corona, and clipped the gorgeous blond in the right shoulder. She screamed and fell on top of me, dropping her gun.

"Hello, wench," the big cowboy smiled.

He grabbed the girl by the back of the neck and began to tie and gag her with my bedsheets, which he stripped out from under me. I rolled into a crack between the bed and the wall and wedged there until I was yanked out by the hair.

Ted backhanded me across the face. He dragged me into the kitchen, where he pushed me into a chair and shoved my face into this story.

"Finish this," he growled, and I did. "And fix this," he added, pointing to his swollen knee, and I did that, too.

After I'd written the sentence with, "Ted's knee got better" in it (this one) he filled his wineskin from my water cooler and went through my cupboards, taking four cans of Hancock Pork 'n' Beans I'd got on sale, six for a dollar.

"Gads, that's expensive," he said, noticing the price tags.

He hefted the girl over his shoulder, and walked out.

"Get me a horse," I heard him call back.

I haven't had many distractions since. An old woman moved into the upstairs apartment, but she moved out again a week later, complaining of drafts and a bizarre infestation of geckoes.

As far as Ted and the woman are concerned... as is often the case in bounty-hunter type stories, they fell in love before Ted could bring her to the hanging, and were married. I haven't heard from either of them since, but maybe it's just as well. Writing about those two was a very painful experience.

*Did I say "The Third Story" was last because I wrote it first? I lied. Pizza Hell was first—and last. I wrote this story at a time when I worked as a waiter at the Pizza Hut in Waterville, Maine. Like so many of my stories, the events in it are impossible, but it gets across the exact feeling of working a busy restaurant shift. If you've ever waited tables, you'll know exactly what that feels like. This is a very old story, but I still love it.*

# PIZZA HELL

It is Friday night, and the air is fraught with possibility. I carry two full buckets of ice to the front of the restaurant and fill the bin. I get no thanks, but you have to be prepared for anything when you're a waiter at an outlet of one of the largest fast food chains in the western world, so I set my jaw and try to think what's next.

There's a line of people near the "hostess will seat you" sign that trails through the foyer and straight out into the parking lot. Sometimes I just want to run up and grab someone by the lapels and scream at them that this is not Epcot Center and there are no rides. I have never done this but there is no guarantee that I will not at any second.

People jostle into me, running to and fro with dirty dishes, pitchers of soda and hot pizzas. One of the cooks shout that they are out of pepperoni. It is all a noisy blur, and I find it hard to concentrate on what I am supposed to be doing. I pull out my check pad for a hint, but am greeted with the sight of about twelve sheets of scribbled on, stapled paper that awake an inner urge to throw them all into the air and shriek at the top of my lungs. Again, I have never done this but I don't know of any bookies who are playing the odds against it. I motor out onto the floor and look at my section, where my customers smile and nod and seem to be having a good time. I find that my smile is still there and in proper working order, so I flash it at them.

Four people sit at the back of my section, examining menus. I power over to them, fishing out a pen and a fresh check.

"Good evening," I say, smiling, "I'm Bill, and I'll be your waiter tonight."

They smile, move their mouths, and make sounds. One of them makes a few sounds that cause them all to laugh, and I join in, laughing appreciatively at I know not what. They want pizza. A large thick crust, no. What's the difference between thick and thin? Which do you like best, Bill? Neither, I don't eat the stuff, it's bad for you. Haha. No, I won't make the funny face like the guy in the add.

I motor back to the kitchen and punch the order in as fast as I can. I see that two of my tables are ready for a box, and the hostess has wiped one off and reset it with four fresh people.

"How you doin' Bill?"

I crack open a real smile for Karen. "O.K. Karen, how 'bout you?"

She rolls her eyes and smiles the 'I am in hell but you know that because so are you' smile.

Someone bumps into me and dislodges me a few inches on the way by. Karen is swept out into the dining room and dissapears amid the chaos. I am about to fill a few cups with ice when I notice the dishwasher, who usually looks pale and drained, stumbling forth from the back hallway with bright red cheeks. His eyes are staring forward like he's just seen a ghost.

"Can somebody change the beer?" Rita yells from behind me. "Bill?"

"I got it," I say, never taking my eyes from the dishwasher.

"Nick," I whisper, and his head snaps up. There is a moment of almost horror in his eyes, then recognition.

"Something wrong with the subfreezer," he mutters, and stumbles past me carrying a sack of ground beef.

"Someone change the beer!" a voice yells, maybe Kelly's. The tone of her voice says that if the beer doesn't get changed soon one of her arms will be ripped off. I don't want that to happen, so I motor to the back hallway and into the walk-in. I have seven-hundred other things to do, but they all suspend when I do a good deed. 'Sorry about the wait,' I can say, 'I was changing the keg.' The customers will smile and nod and tell me it's o.k.

I change the kegs too fast and spray Michelob Light all over my shirt and apron. It's polyester, so the liquid beads up and rolls off as if I was a newly waxed car. Boom! They're changed, it's back out to bring the drinks to party 1, boxes to parties 2 and 3, check on 4, 5, 6, 7, and 8, and take number 9's order. I motor out front and bump into the manager, who smiles like an idiot because he has his back to the 40 foot long line of people who are waiting to be seated, and is headed out back to do paperwork during the rush. After I have forgotten the incident and am well on my way, his voice calls me back.

"Bill."

I whirl.

"Yeah?"

"We need some pepperoni."

My mind shrieks like a shifting pile of rusted out cars which are about to topple on and kill a squirrel.

"Jim I'm," I say, "I'm busy, I-"

"We all are, Bill," he says, and smiles and claps me amiably on the shoulder. Then he starts to whistle "Dock of the Bay," and heads out back to sit down.

I positively tear up the tile on my way out back, where I pull open the walk-in door and rush inside. There is no pepperoni to be seen. A friday night, I'm busier than hell and oh boy, no pepperoni has been thawed. The door to the sub-freezer is there, nestled between the cucumbers and the beer kegs, and without thinking I grab the colder than cold steel handle and yank it open.

A wall of cold fog rolls out and hits me square. I take a step back, blink, and behold a sight stranger than even the time the drunk driver parked his car through booths b-4 and 5.

Now I have never liked the subfreezer, because it is cramped and cold enough to freeze your eyelids open in a matter of minutes. The cooling unit (a thing on the cieling that looks like R2-D2) and everything within three feet of it is covered with a thick flow of ice. To make things worse, the subfreezer has a habit of locking people inside. But this...

The sub freezer isn't there anymore. It has been replaced with what I suppose I should describe as a howling void. I stare into it for awhile, and it stares back for a moment before I slam the door shut again.

"Jesus" I say, and run out of the walk-in.

I try desperately to find the dishwasher, but he is nowhere to be found and the hostess will absolutely not stop telling me how many new parties I have and she stuffs four or five slips of paper into my apron. They are all drink orders, but I do not look at them. Instead I power out into the dining room, where I can see the manager explaining something to one of my customers.

"Hi Bill," he smiles fakely, "what's the matter, huh? These people are waiting for their waiter. Is this your section?"

I smile weakly at the people, who glare back like I've just dug up their lawn with an A.T.C.

"I've got a problem, Jim," I say, trying to keep from turning into jelly.

"Well so do I, Bill. These people here are getting kind of hungry."

"Seriously," I say. "I need to see you out back."

The manager grins obsequiously at the customers, who glare back like he's just taken a turn on the A.T.C.

"Okay," he says to me. "Take their order and come out back when you get a second."

I take their order, trying to smile and be helpful and not open scream my lungs out, then I make my way back through the throng to the kitchen and then through the back hall and into the office. Still no sign of the dishwasher.

"What's the problem, Bill?" says the manager, standing with arms akimbo.

"There's something wrong with the sub-freezer."

He looks at me funny. "Like what?" he says.

"It's..." I find I can't tell him, so I settle for explaining that we are out of pepperoni.

"Well," he says, smiling, "then we're out of pepperoni."

I tell him it isn't the pepperoni. It's the subfreezer and there's something really wrong with it. He throws up his hands and says, "what am I supposed to do about it? Call a repairman for Pete's sake! I don't know anything about subfreezers! Deal with it! Come on, people."

With that he walks out front again. By now I could care less about my parties, but on the outside chance that I am only going insane I truck it out front and fill some drinks. I have a tray full, plus a pitcher in my right hand and a stack of ice-filled cups teetering out of my left apron pocket. Liquids slosh over the rims of numerous pitchers and cups as I deliver everything, and now I find that my smile is broken. The most I can manage is a pathetic grin.

A few of my customers make blunt comments about the service, and I apologize and tell them their meals should be ready in a few minutes, looking up and getting a shock when I see that my light is on. Back to the kitchen I go, where I see that the cut table is filled with pizzas tagged with slips marked Bill, Bill, Bill, Bill.

I grab two large pans which I have no idea where they are going and look around for the hostess to ask her for help. She is nowhere to be seen, and one of the cooks is missing.

"Come on!" the shift supervisor, Angie, whines at me. "They're getting cold!"

Rrrahh! I bring them all out to the wrong tables and tell the customers to enjoy their meal. One lady asks for more coffee, a man in an adjacent booth for napkins, and everyone asks for straws and silverware. Two people hand me credit cards and I nearly step on a little girl on my way back to the kitchen, where I notice the dishwasher sobbing behind the oven.

"Nick!" I say, edging in beside him. "Nick, pull it together, man! I saw it, too!"

He is incoherent and mutters something about Fred Astaire.

"What," I ask, trying to comprehend. "The dancer?"

He shakes his head furiously and shrieks "NO NO NO THE CLAYMATION VERSION FROM THE CHRISTMAS SPECIAL" and I pull him out from behind the oven and drag him out back beyond earshot of the customers. I settle him down in the dish room and tell him to stay put until I come back, only now he won't let go of my arm and keeps whining for his mother.

"What's the problem?" the manager asks, rounding the corner like a hyena sensing a weakness. I turn on him, wrenching my arm free from the useless dishwasher.

"I'll tell you what the problem is," I yell, storming toward him. "Your subfreezer is an infinite vacuum and no one in this place gives a shit!"

My tie-raid is punctuated by a piercing scream as one of the cooks bolts out of the walk in and streaks across the room, continuing straight out through the back door.

The manager looks from me to the back door to the walk in and back to me again. He starts for the walk-in and I tag along. When we reach the subfreezer door he gives me a worried look, and I shrug, wanting him to see. He pulls open the door.

The subfreezer is back. He steps reluctantly inside, looks around, and reemerges with a box of frozen pepperoni.

"I'd like to see you later," he tells me on his way out.

The freezer door has swung shut and I instinctively reach out and open it up. Banjo music pops out, and I am looking at an old western town. A man with an unkempt beard and crumpled hat waves and nods from where he is playing his banjo on the wooden sidewalk, and I slam the door.

"Jesus," I say, and motor out of there.

I go out front, where things are breaking like a weak dam. The line of customers has gridlocked traffic in the parking lot, and a few of my parties have walked out. What remaining waitstaff there are comment to me as they walk by and ask if I need any help, and when I say yes they say they have their own problems. One of the cooks has left, and the pizzas are taking an unreasonably long time. A short man peers over the counter and asks me where the hell his credit card is. I put my hand behind my ear and say "What's that shorty? Need a booster seat?"

The man gasps and I head for the back, where I pick up the phone book and start to leaf through the yellow pages to find someone who works on Frez-Fast subfreezer units, thinking what else can I do.

Jimi's Refrigeration Repair
If It's Not Cool
We'll Fix It

The ad lists a number of manufacturers, including Frez-Fast, so I reach for the phone, which rings before I can grab it.

"Hello?"

"Two-Rivers Pizza Wheel?"

"Yeah, Bill speaking."

"Bill, this is Nina, the district manager. Is Jim there?"

"Yeah but he's busy," I lie, wanting to use the phone.

"Well have him call me. Bill, what's going on up there?"

"How do you mean?"

"Our phone's ringing off the hook down here. We've got so many complaints about you guys tonight we're starting to worry about you."

"We had a problem with the freezer but it's under control now," I lie. I hang up the phone before she can protest and I dial the number for Jimi's Refrigeration Repair.

"'Lo."

"Hello, Jimi?"

"Yep."

"I've- I'm Bill Parks at Two-Rivers Pizza Wheel and I aha... need someone to come over and fix our Frez-Fast."

"'Kay."

"When can you- can you do it now?"

"Yep."

"Oh, o.k. thanks, ah - Jimi."

"Bye."

I hang up and turn around just in time to see two cooks dissapear into the walk in. I shout but it is too late, and when I open the walk in door they are gone. I contemplate my choices and a few seconds later the manager walks past me.

"Pete and James go in here?" he asks.

"Yeah but-"

"Thanks." He opens the door and we are greeted with racks piled high with cartons and sacks of low grade meat. Jim shakes his head and gives me a weird look on his way out.

I do not open it.

I do go out front, and find that all twelve of my parties have left either without paying or before ordering and have been replaced with twelve new ones, all expectantly holding menus. The short man is pointing at me, screaming to the manager about his credit card. I untie my apron and fling it into the middle of the dining room. All of the cooks are now gone, along with the hostess and two waitresses. Karen runs up and asks me what the hell is going on.

"Come on," I say, but before I can grab her arm a customer does and he drags her into the crowd, yelling something that I cannot hear into her face. A few of the people in the line begin to yell things at me and I run back behind the latticework, pursued at first by just a few and then by the entire mob. I round the corner and slip on a tomato slice, nearly falling into the oven and trying desperately to remove my uniform. They are jumping over the counter now and I dart into the back hallway just as one of them throws the cash register at my head. It explodes harmlessly against a wall, and I pull the dishwasher to his feet and begin to drag him for the back door. Right away I see this is no good as a waiter bolts in from outside pursued by the mob, which has found the rear entrance. He tries to go out front but is set upon by the cash register group, who begin to rip his clothes off.

I am surrounded, and it occurs to me that I'll have to make a break for the walk-in. An old lady grabs hold of the dishwasher's hair and I am forced to beat her off with a nearby can of chunk pineapple. I pull the walk-in door open with a free hand and pull the senseless dishwasher inside.

The subfreezer door is closed, and I yank it quickly open and shove the dishwasher inside, leaping after him as a large man tears the shirt from my back. Then the door slams shut behind us and we are on a rocky mountaintop with an icy wind howling all around. And me in polyester pants and no shirt. The dishwasher snaps out of it after a few months and we set up a nice farm in the valley, where the foot-long mosquitos bother us but not as much as a lack of food. Nick makes a pet of one of them and uses it to make orange juice. We are alone for a few years until one day a short bald man in blue coveralls happens upon our home.

"Bill?" he says. "Bill Parks?"

I nod, dumbfounded.

"Jimi Pinnette!"

"Jimi?" I say, pointing frantically. "Jimi's Refrigeration Repair!"

He nods and says he likes our setup.

"Nice log cabins," he comments.

"Yeah, Jimi, what the hell happened? How did you get here?'

"Who's this?" says Nick, who has been washing the wooden plates.

"Jimi," says Jimi, extending his hand.

"Hi," says Nick. "Nick."

Jimi says he can't stay for long because he has to get back and make some calls.

"Back?" I say. "Back to Two Rivers?"

He says yes and starts to leave, but I don't let him. Not without us, he doesn't go back. He says okay and I start to pack our stuff but Nick wants to stay here.

"Things are simpler here," he tells me stroking his mosquito, who buzzes affectionately. "Anyway I have to take care of Jake."

After a certain amount of arguing I finally concede to let him stay, and I follow Jimi to the mountaintop, where he uses a crowbar to open a crack in the sky.

We go through, and are back in the walk-in at Pizza Wheel. He indicates the door hinges and explains, "Here's yer problem. It wasn't the cooling unit at all. It was the door hinges."

When I tell him I don't understand, he says, "what's in a box before you open it?"

I tell him I don't know.

"Exactly," he says triumphantly. "But once you open them, boxes have the courtesy to manifest their insides into something at least that's plausible. Not so with some of these new doors they're comin' out with. Especially it's the hinges. Can you sign for the bill?"

I tell him it's the least I can do and walk out front afterwards to see what's what. The place is a shambles. Dough, cheese, and pizza sauce are everywhere. The conveyor oven has been tipped over and it looks like someone has tried to open the safe with a prybar. I wonder if it was Jimi.

I pull up some police line tape and walk out into the dining room, which looks like it has been through a hurricane. My apron lies under the "Hostess Will Seat You" sign, covered with broken glass. I pick it up and dust it off as the phone rings.

"Hello?"

"Hello, Two-Rivers Pizza Wheel?"

"Yeah, Bill speaking."

"Bill, this is Nina, the district manager."

"Hi Nina."

"Hi, is Jim there?"

"No, I don't, ah-"

"Well tell him we heard about what happened tonight and we're very angry down here. We fully expect you guys to open as scheduled in the morning."

"I'll tell him," I say, and hang up the phone.

# AFTERWORD

So that's it. That's all she wrote. I have hundreds—maybe thousands of other stories in my plastic basement bins and hard drives, if you're ever interested. But I'm pretty sure these are the cream of the crop. I really need to thank my parents, who let me grow up under the influence of the *Twilight Zone* and *Sesame Street* and *Monty Python,* and who bought me books like *The Hitchhiker's Guide to the Galaxy* and games like *Dungeons and Dragons.* All those things warped and changed me in fun ways, and I'm eternally grateful.

I'm glad you and I got to share these stories, too. I hope you enjoyed reading them, and that they'll warp and change you, too, in good ways, of course. I guess there's not much more to say. Until we meet again somewhere, sometime. Adieu.

# ACKNOWLEDGEMENTS

I have to thank my mom, the incomparable Jeanne Gerencer, for buying me one weird science fiction or fantasy book after another for years while I was growing up. I don't know how she picked them, but she had some kind of source, because they were all excellent. I owe a massive debt to Robert Sheckley, astounding SF & F humorist, both for writing so many of the stories I love, and for answering my pathetic email years ago and then becoming my friend. I also owe an obvious debt to Douglas Adams, whose Hitchhiker series I read so many times they fell apart and I repeatedly had to buy new copies. While on a Watson Fellowship to study radio theatre in London for a year, I actually tracked him down at his house. He was so gracious. He invited me in and gave me a beer and talked to me about his work. I even got to see the manuscript of his first book in typewritten form. And finally, to all the people who've been kind to me over the years. There are so many. Thank you.

# ABOUT THE AUTHOR

## Tom Gerencer

Tom Gerencer started writing science fiction and fantasy humor at a young age. He has been published in several online and print publications over the years, including Realms of Fantasy, Science Fiction Age, and Galaxy's Edge. His work has been translated into Russian, French, K'naag, and German, and has appeared in anthologies such as The Mammoth Book of Comic Fantasy and I, Alien. Tom has been privileged to have great writing teachers and mentors in his past, including the incredibly kind Mike Resnick and the astounding comic genius Robert Sheckley. Tom makes his living from nonfiction writing, and subscribes to the belief that you have to write a million words of bunk before you write one good one. His first was "cucumber," and he was exceptionally proud of it. Tom lives in West Virginia with his wife Kathy, sons Maddox and Ben, and two ornery dogs.

Made in the USA
Middletown, DE
02 July 2021